TRACE

IKE KEEN

Paperback-Press
an imprint of A & S Publishing
A & S Holmes, Inc.

ISBN: 0692228551
ISBN-13: 978-0-69222855-5

DEDICATION

To my wife Raynell who pushed and prodded me till this book was done. Thank you for your patience.

TABLE OF CONTENTS

DEDICATION..iii
ACKNOWLEDGMENTS..i
In the Beginning..1
Chapter 1 5
Chapter 2...13
Chapter 3...16
Chapter 4...20
Chapter 5...25
Chapter 6...31
Chapter 7...34
Chapter 8...38
Chapter 9...45
Chapter 10...49
Chapter 11...52
Chapter 12...57
Chapter 13...63
Chapter 14...69
Chapter 15...72
Chapter 16...74
Chapter 17...78
Chapter 18...83
Chapter 19...91
Chapter 20...94
Chapter 21...96
Chapter 22...99
Chapter 23... 102
Chapter 24... 110
Chapter 25... 115
Chapter 26... 118
Chapter 27... 121
Chapter 28... 124
Chapter 29... 130
Chapter 30... 134
Chapter 31... 140
Chapter 32... 143
Chapter 33... 150
Chapter 34... 155
Chapter 35... 158
Chapter 36... 167
Chapter 37... 172
Chapter 38... 174
Chapter 39... 178
Chapter 40... 181
Chapter 41... 185
Chapter 42... 191
ABOUT THE AUTHOR.. 193

ACKNOWLEDGMENTS

I would also like to thank Sharon my editor who showed me the ins and outs of making a story a good read and to Sleuth's ink that without their support I would still be just pecking away on a keyboard.

IN THE BEGINNING

Things had been pretty slow the past few weeks. My PI business, Max Black Inc., was at a standstill and my friend Pat, chief of the detectives with the Springfield PD, was doing more paper work than he liked. Catch up work he called it and he said there was a hell of a lot of it.

Oh, the usual stuff was still in vogue, bar fights and winos keeping the beat cops busy, but nothing big. The last case we had worked on together was a rackets scheme. A couple of outsiders had moved in and were hustling some of the store owners on the square, roughing up a couple of them because they wouldn't pay.

It was a good thing we put the nix on them before Sampson got a hold of them, Sampson being the local organized crime boss here in the Queen city. His boys would have done more than arrested them, if you get my drift.

I was with Pat at Benny's Diner eating supper, discussing Sampson when I heard the phone ring; Benny answered it and looked our way. He nodded, hung up, then waltzed over to the table and leaned in close. His low tone made it evident he didn't want everyone in the joint to hear what he had to say.

"The PD's been looking all over town for you. Said you need to get to the river as quick as you can. There's something you need to see."

I noticed the two reporters from the Ledger sat about two feet away. Benny was trying to play it cool so they wouldn't get wind of what was going on. Like it would matter since they have ears as big as an elephant's and noses that can smell out a story when it is brewing.

Pat turned to me. "You want to tag along?"

"Why not, nothing better to do at the moment." So we left, Pat paid the bill as I kept my eye on the reporters who were watching us real close. As we walked past the windows, I nudged Pat and nodded toward the inside. Both of them were already making tracks toward the register and Benny stalled them off so we could get away.

The night was hot, especially by the river. The temperature hadn't dropped much, hovering between the upper eighties and lower nineties, and the humidity was thick, almost like breathing the river itself. Doc Pace was giving the body the once over when we got there. He and his assistant had laid it on a rubber tarp. The only way you could tell the body was female was by the shoes she had on—ankle straps and open toed high heels. The rope keeping her tied down had covered them and kept the fishes from nibbling at them.

Pat was over talking to the two kids wrapped in blankets, who had found her. I figured they were having a midnight swim, among other things, and this midnight swim would be with them for a long time.

"Not much to go on." Pace stood and stripped the rubber gloves from his hands. "Just the shoes. The rest of her is pretty much gone ID-wise, so unless I can get some prints or she had had dental work done here in the city…"

I saw that most of the flesh had been stripped from her

face and she was bloated. Other bits of flesh hung loose like thin strings from other places on her body and her eyes were gone. "Any idea how long she's been down there?"

"Hard to tell," he shrugged, "Maybe two, three weeks, probably more like a month from the way the fish have been at her. Most of the flesh has been stripped off her face and she is bloated." I looked at her again and grimaced, the bits of flesh hanging loose and her missing eyes made my supper turn sour.

"Those two kids, they the ones who found her?" I jerked a thumb behind me.

"Yeah, a couple of lovers, they decided to have a little midnight swim in the buff and lover boy dove under to surprise his true love and got a surprise himself."

I bit back a crude remark pertaining to surprises, pulled a cigar out of my shirt pocket, lit up and watched Doc's assistant wrap the body up, his face pale and his gag reflex weak. Pat wandered over after talking with the two youngsters; he shook his head and chuckled.

I took a deep draw then blew the smoke out. "What's funny?" He stepped up beside me. "Those two." He made one last entry in his notebook and then shoved it in his coat pocket. "When I asked the guy about what he saw under the water he told me it sure wasn't what he expected to see."

"What about the girl?"

"She didn't see anything; she was too busy dragging her boyfriend to the bank to keep him from drowning. She said he was screaming like a girl and thrashing around as she pulled him in. That was when the argument started. I don't think he'll be seeing her again."

I snickered and looked out at the river. The moonlight shining on it made it look like black glass, it was so still. There were no night sounds, just a deep quiet, or should I say dead quiet. Yeah, dead quiet; the crickets, frogs and other night creatures knew what had happened and were reverently silent.

I shivered and walked to where Pat was talking to Doc by the coroner's wagon. Doc told him he would do what he could to ID the body but couldn't guarantee anything.

As the wagon pulled away, I spotted the two reporters from the diner running toward us. Pat groaned and shook his head. I stepped back as they skidded to a halt in front of him, both babbling questions a mile a minute.

Pat listened, but his only answer was, "No comment."

I chuckled and walked back toward Pat's car. He glanced back over his shoulder and gave me a dirty look as I leaned against the fender, waiting for the two reporters to run out of steam and give it up so we could leave.

CHAPTER 1

I sat at my girlfriend/secretary Shelly's desk and watched the sun beat down on the pavement on Commercial Street. Wave after wave of heat shimmered into the already heated air, only disturbed when a car passed by, then it returned.

Not many people were out, but those that were, were dressed in as little as decently legal, the younger ones anyway. The older gals were dressed as if it were early spring, the chill not quite having left the air yet. I have a hunch they were sweating like horses after a good run.

Once before we had had a heat wave like this back in '39, just before Hitler decided he wanted more than just Germany under his belt. That one had lasted from July to almost October, then it turned cold and the snow came. Like they say, you don't like the weather in the Ozarks just wait a minute, it will change.

I was mulling over last night in my mind. The way the girl was murdered smacked of execution style; someone knew too much and was silenced for it. I remember a couple of years back when one of Sampson's boys had flipped on him; he agreed to testify against the big guy for immunity. He was under fed protection but Sampson's boys still got him, weighted him down like the girl and tossed him to the fish. But nothing like that was in the works that I knew of, Sampson laying low after that. No, something else was going on and I was gonna let Pat take care of it because it was probably nothing more than a husband tired of his wife cheating on him.

I leaned back in my chair to where the fan could blow on me, the air hot but it was air,(me) mentally cussing Cooney out about the fan, not this one but the exhaust fan on the roof. It had busted a couple of days ago and Reggie Cooney and I were still battling about getting it fixed.

It wasn't air conditioning but at least it kept the air moving in the building and made it a little more comfortable. I had just gotten off the phone with him as Cooney owns this building and a few others on Commercial Street; most of them from what I could gather have non-working exhaust fans or none at all.

Usually, his help comes around and does the upkeep on the buildings and Cooney sits back and rakes in the green. But since the war his two men were overseas and he had to do it himself, which meant sometime before winter hit. He told me he would get to me when he could, that he was having trouble getting parts because of the war and that I would just have to grin and bear it like all the other patriotic citizens were doing. I told him bluntly that till it was fixed, he got nothing in the way of rent.

"I'll throw your ass out if you do that," Cooney threatened on the phone.

"Uh-huh and I'll just put a bug in the city building inspectors ear about those foundations you haven't fixed yet under a certain building he inspected a while back," I said, grinning.

There was a pause on the line and then I heard him cuss under his breath. In said building a corner of the floor had given way because the foundation had cracked and part of it fell into the basement. Cooney had shored up the floor and swore he would get it fixed as soon as possible. That was a year ago.

"Besides," I continued, "Shelly doesn't take the heat too well and sometimes she comes in to work wearing just enough to keep her legal." That was more of a lie than the truth. Shelly dresses comfortably and decent for the public.

"Well now," his voice brightened a little, "I might be able to do something. How about Thursday if I can get the parts. Shouldn't take more than a couple of hours. She'll be there Thursday won't she? I mean one of you will be there?"

I grunted and told him one of us would be here and hung up. Cooney is a dirty old man and Shelly caught him looking up her dress one day while he was fixing a lower wall socket next to her desk. She had gave him thunder over it and to tell you the truth, I wouldn't have guessed Shelly knew as many ear burning words as those she threw at him. Cooney stood there and took it, what else was he going to do? Shelly is one mean woman if you cross her, and she's fine looking.

I've known Shelly for a while, met her back when she worked in Benny's Diner. I knew she liked me then, always coming to make sure everything was alright, slipping me an extra piece of pie or just coming by and refreshing my coffee just so she could talk to me. Back then, it made me a little nervous, I mean, I wasn't in the mood for a dame under foot all the time. Then she stopped by the office one day, a friend of hers told her to let me see her dressed like a woman and not a waitress, and I was hooked.

Tall and leggy, she stands about 5' 8" in her bare feet. Sugar-maple colored hair falls in soft waves to her shoulders and surrounds her oval face, high cheek bones and a cute little chin. Her lips are luscious and full and those lips are irresistible. Her curves are in all the right places and she knows how to dress to show them just enough to make me happy and honest. Yep, she is a living doll and she is *my* living doll.

I stood, grabbed my hat, then stepped out into the blast furnace heat and locked the door. The sun was already half into its noon time run and the shade was slowly disappearing, the sidewalk heated up and burned through the soles of my shoes as I walked.

A couple of kids darted past me, their bare feet slapped the sidewalk as they ran. I could remember those times when we shed our shoes the first warm spell, and before the summer was over our feet were calloused and as tough as leather. Now, just the thought of it made me cringe.

I slung my suit jacket over my shoulder, walked past Booneville Street down to Al's cigar shop. I hustled because I knew he had air conditioning, something of a rarity in this town. It cost him a little more on his lease but it was worth it for his customers who came all the way from the Square to shoot the breeze and enjoy the coolness.

I opened the door and a bell jingled, a blast of arctic air hit me as I stepped inside. Al's shop was right between the Citizen's Bank and the five and dime. It had once been a barber shop.

The fellow that owned it then ran a numbers business out of the upstairs till the feds nailed him. The shop sat vacant for a few years. It was just the right size for what Al was doing. Glass cases ran along the three walls in the shop, each one filled with pipes, cigars or pipe tobacco. I breathed in deep to savor the aromas. I could live here.

Cuban, and Mexican cigars as dark as night, pipe tobaccos that hinted of men in suits talking of business deals or sitting in one of those gentlemen's clubs, reading papers or looking over old books to remember times when they were young, exploring a world still wild and untamed.

"Hello Max, Cooney get your fan fixed yet?"

I jumped a bit and Al chuckled. "Nope, I guess I'm going to have to threaten to shoot the S.O.B. if he doesn't."

I picked up a cigar and studied it.

The once Captain of Detectives in this town was over six feet, his hair white and thin on top. He had a scar along his left jaw line, picked up from the last encounter which had caused his retirement. But his face is solid, with a square chin, a rugged nose underneath which sat a white mustache, waxed and curled on the ends. His eyes are green and still have that drilling stare in them from his police days.

"How's Shelly doing?" He leaned on the counter.

"She's fine, feisty as ever."

"Good. By the way, a couple of fellows were in here just a few minutes ago. Wanted to know where you bunked, as they put it. You might have passed them on the street."

I shook my head no, but strangers looking for me, *usually* meant trouble in this profession. However, as long as the money was good and they didn't want me to do anything illegal, I could handle it. I bought some cigars, shot the breeze for a bit, said my goodbyes and went back out, breaking a sweat almost before I opened the door.

As I headed back, I noticed two guys looking into my office window, pressing up against the glass with their hands on either side of their faces to see if anyone was in. One was tall and lanky, the other short and a little heavy. I was sure they were the guys Al told me about.

"Can I help you gentlemen?" I had walked up pretty quiet on them and they both jumped, the tall one reached for his left armpit then dropped his hand. I clamped a cigar between my teeth.

He cleared his throat. "You Max Black?"

I nodded and they looked at each other and smiled. You could tell they were from somewhere besides here, their accent trying to sound Southern, but underneath it was an Eastern twang. They were dressed in light clothes; the lanky one wore tan slacks and a thin white shirt, the heavy one darker slacks and an off-white shirt. Both wore new fedoras. The fat one was constantly taking his off and wiping out the sweat band with a soggy hanky.

"One and the same." I unlocked the door and opened it. I ushered them in and nodded to the two chairs in front of Shelly's desk, commenting on how it was cooler here than back in my office, which had no windows.

"Name's Orville Gates." The tall man gestured toward the other guy. "This is my brother, Chet." Orville stuck out his hand as he eased into one of the chairs.

He had a strong grip, a working man's grip, but it lacked the callousness of the working man's hands. Chet's grasp was limp, his hands even softer. I started to grin when he sat down. The chair groaned and his butt hung over the sides. He gave me a questioning look and I snapped my attention to Orville to keep him from seeing the grin that was forming on my face.

"Always get this hot here in the summer?" Chet's voice was softer than his brother's and had a little angry edge to it, "We live in the mountains, hot as hell during the day but the nights cool off right nice."

"The mountains?" With each movement the large man made, the chair groaned a death keel. It was amusing.

"We're from Kentucky, Mr. Black." Chet wiped sweat from his brow.

My gaze jumped back to Orville so I wouldn't out right laugh at poor Chet's distress. "Long way from home boys, what can I do for you?"

Orville pulled an envelope from his shirt pocket. It was folded in half, so he straightened it out with his hands till it was flat. He took his time, slowly smoothing it till he had it just right before he laid it on my desk.

"We would like for you to find our sister, Becky Gates," he said, "Her picture and two hundred dollars are in there."

I picked up the envelope and opened it. Inside were two, one hundred dollar bills and a photo. I pulled the photo out and looked at it, then at them. The family resemblance wasn't there. The girl was prettier. She didn't have the long nose and high forehead that Orville had nor did she have any weight on her like Chet did. I guess when she was conceived; the gene pool tossed out the ugly and fat and kept the pretty and curvy.

Her face was a heart shape and her lips were full, very kissable and had a slight pout to them. Even in the plain dress you could tell she was stacked. She had pretty eyes, eyes I had seen somewhere before. Funny how that happens isn't it, I mean you see someone and swear you have seen them before when you haven't. This time though I was sure she was familiar.

I started to toss the picture back on my desk, then stopped. I pulled it closer and looked at her shoes. I couldn't be sure, but they looked vaguely like the shoes on the dead girl. Till I was sure, I'd keep my mouth shut.

"So what makes you think she is here?" I asked leaning back in my chair, watching the two closely.

"Well, we have some cousins who live here, or lived here, haven't heard from them in a coon's age. We figured she may have come out here to live with them." Orville sat back in his chair. "We had sort of a family disagreement when daddy passed on and she, well, she just up and left. Ain't heard from her since."

I tossed the picture on the desk and watched them for a minute. Orville was the cool one, sitting with his arms folded across his chest, waiting. Chet was fooling with the crease of his pants, glancing from me to Orville. Something more than a missing sister reflected in his eyes.

"Ok," I leaned forward on the desk, "I'll check around and see what I can come up with. Where you staying?"

"The Missouri Hotel, room 204," Orville said standing, "You need more money…."

"This will do for a start," I picked up the envelope and pulling out the two hundreds. "I'll get in touch if I find out anything."

"Much appreciated," Orville stood and stuck out his hand.

Chet hoisted off the chair and did the same, but his hand was sweating; it was like shaking a limp noodle. Orville jerked his head toward the door and the two of them left. Once outside they began to talk, Chet shaking his head as Orville said something, both of them in deep conversation as they disappeared from the view of the window.

I picked up the picture again and studied it. If those two were kin to the girl in the picture, I was kin to George Washington. No, something else was brewing and I would find out what once I found this Becky Gates. If they had lied to me... well, I don't like to be lied to, and they would find out the penalty for it, which wasn't a nice thing at all.

And if it is the dead girl? I shook my head, no, my gut told me that the dead girl and the one in the picture wasn't the same but I could be wrong. I had a buddy who was a photographer and I would soon pay him a visit to see if the shoes in the picture were the same ones on the decease.

I slipped the photo in my shirt pocket along with the money and walked out of the office, locked the door and crossed the street where I parked my old heap, a '39 Ford Coupe. I crawled in and cranked the starter over. The old Ford fired up. I pulled out and turned east toward Jefferson Street, picking up as much speed as the old car could muster and making some air to cool me down as I headed toward City Hospital and the morgue.

CHAPTER 2

The Morgue is in the City Hospital basement, the entrance sometimes confused with the Emergency Room entrance by the drunks who stagger in after a fight and need patching up. I bet that's a real kicker when one of them staggers in and sees nothing but dead bodies lying around. I pulled the door open and cool air came out, along with the smell of disinfectant and the faint smell of bodily fluids. Let me tell you, not my favorite place.

Doc was in the main room by himself, working on the girl's body when I walked in. I eased my way toward him, the room quiet as a tomb, the only sounds being his muttering and the clink of his tools. I was almost on him when he straightened up and turned toward me, a scalpel in one hand and a bloody saw in the other. He reminded me of a mad scientist trying to bring the dead back to life.

"When are you guys gonna learn I know when you are here?" He turned and laid the saw and scalpel on the tray beside him.

"Doesn't mean we can't try," I walked over to him. His last assistant, a young fellow with a sense of humor, had tried sneaking up on Doc when he worked with him but it was of no use, Doc always knew he was there. He told me he figured the old man must have sonar because he was supposed to be hard of hearing, supposed to be.

"Did you get a print off of her," I kept my eyes off the dead body, which was already laid open. Another reason I don't like coming down here.

"One."

He moved a little to the side and shot me a sideways glance and a knowing grin. The old bastard.

"Pat is running the print now. It might be a few days though. Why?"

I reached in my pocket, pulled out the picture and handed it to him. Doc scanned the image then handed it back.

"It might be her, the hair is the same color and if we had her eyes...."

"What about her shoes?" I said, pointing at the picture.

Doc took the photo back and gave it a closer look, grunted then took it over to a table and picked up a magnifying glass. He moved it back and forth over the picture.

"They could be the same." His eyes were still locked on the photo. "I can't be certain, though."

I took the picture and the glass and tried it myself. He was right, you couldn't be certain. The picture looked as if it had been taken in the late evening, the shadows darkening around her feet.

"Anything else?" I laid the magnifying glass down.

"Well, she was dead before she was dumped," Doc said, "Stabbed in the heart, one thrust, on her left side between her ribs."

"So why toss her in the river?"

"Did you see the way she was tied down? If that kid hadn't found her she would have been picked clean and her bones settled to the bottom for someone years from now to find."

"What do you mean the way she was tied down?"

"Besides stabbing her, they drove a steel spike through her ankles, then used steel cables to tie her to the concrete block. Oh, she might have popped up a few years from now, but in a lot worse shape than she is now. She was meant to be under for a long time."

"Thanks Doc," I turned to walk away.

"Yeah and don't light up till you get outside; this place is a bomb waiting for a match to set it off."

I paused for a moment, and stopped myself from pulling out a cigar and lighting up. Like I said, the old man must have sonar or is physic.

Once outside, I lit up as I walked back to my car, drawing in deep to get the smell out of my lungs and nose. I sat in the car for a few minutes, wondering what the Gates boys, if that was who they really were, would say if it was her. But for some reason my gut told me again it wasn't and for now I was going with my gut.

I held the cigar between my teeth and fired up the old heap again. This time the bomb backfired and got a squeal out of a couple of nurses going inside the hospital. I grinned and shoved the car in gear, pulled out and headed back to Commercial Street and Shelly.

CHAPTER 3

Shelly's house sat out east on Commercial, past the railroad tracks and the Sherman paint warehouse. This is where the business section ended and the residential section started. A few business owners had tried to buy the land the houses sat on a few years back but had failed, one going as far as to offer twice what the property was worth. And in those times, that would have kept a family in high cotton for a long time. It was a no go and the city remained where it was.

Shelly's place used to belong to an old lady who had lived there since the 1890s. The house was a simple clapboard job that lacked the luxuries most homes have in them now. Al helped Shelly and Jack, her twin brother, buy the house when the old lady passed, loaned them the money from his savings and told them to pay it back when they could.

Al even helped them work on the old house, the outside of the structure being not in too bad a shape, but the insides needing a lot of work. Shelly told me there was no indoor bathroom so part of the bigger bedroom was walled off and a bathroom installed with pluming for running water both hot and cold.

Shelly told me about the outhouse they had had to use before the bathroom was done, how Jack had warned her about looking before she sat down. Snakes sometimes occupied the facilities and he didn't want her to get snake bit. She said she held it till she got to work and one morning almost didn't make it. Shelly told one of the waitresses what Jack had told her and the woman laughed her ass off. The woman said it was an old wives tale and he was pulling her leg.

I had to laugh, myself, and she whacked me one, telling me it wasn't funny; she could have had kidney damage from waiting so long. That made me laugh even harder. She didn't speak to me for two days.

The front yard had a big oak tree that shaded almost the entire house, and the back was a pretty good sized, well shaded lot, the property ending at the road tracks that curved behind the house. There were flower beds in both front and back yards. I teased her and told her when Jack came back she better warn him not to mistake them for weeds when he cut the lawn. She told me he already had and that's why she had the neighbor kid do it.

I pulled into the drive and cut my motor, the old engine ticking as it cooled off in the shade of the drive. Shelly was sitting on the front porch on a wicker settee she had bought just for us. I watched her for a few moments as I finished my cigar. She was some gal, a doll that could have had better than me if she wanted.

Now, I'm not an ugly fellow of fifty by no means, but I have a lot of wear on this old mug, a few scars that have been acquired in past cases and a nose that has been broken so many times the doctors in the emergency room run a pool while I am on each case, betting on how many times I will show up with a busted nose.

I watched her stand as I sat there, uncoiling from the

settee, her long legs folding out and onto the wooden flooring of the porch. She wore a pair of white shorts that accented her tanned legs perfectly. Her blouse was a pale green, buttoned up part way and then tied under her breasts.

My Kitten.

I tossed the dead stub of my cigar out the window and crawled out. Her hand shaded her eyes, a smile crossed her face. I walked to the front steps, mounted them and went to her. She fell into my arms and she kissed me sweet and long. Then we sat down, a hot, light breeze blowing over us as she snuggled up close, the heat from her more enjoyable than the heat scorching the air.

"I was listening to the radio," she said holding my hand, "Weather man says it's already passed the 100 mark. I was about to call you and tell you to get your behind out here and enjoy the shade."

"Thanks for thinking of me," I said kissing her on the forehead, "But I got a job, two boys from Kentucky want me to locate their sister. I just hope to hell it isn't the girl that was found in the river."

"Something tells me you don't think it is?" She said looking up at me, "You have that look in your eyes."

"Yeah, well." I shrugged then took the photo out of my shirt pocket and looked at it for a few moments before I handed it to her. "Have you ever seen her before?"

She took it, and a frown crossed her face as she studied the image.

"She looks familiar." Shelly glanced at me and handed it back.

I nodded and took the photo. "You've seen her before?"

"Yeah, but where I can't remember."

"Maybe she worked for Benny?"

"I would have recognized her instantly; no, somewhere else."

"What about Cully's?"

"Maybe, I don't know, it's her eyes that look familiar."

"Yeah." I put the picture back in my pocket. "Those are one of the identifying pieces of the puzzle that are missing."

Shelly shivered and I patted her on the leg. "I'll check around after supper and see if anything pops."

"After supper huh?" She met my gaze and a seductive smile crossed her lips.

"Yeah, unless you got something else in mind" I stood and pulled her up. She giggled and we went inside closing the front door to enjoy the rest of the evening.

CHAPTER 4

The heat was still there when I stepped out on the porch at six o'clock the next morning. The thermometer in the shade of the porch read eighty six. I sipped my coffee and enjoyed the breeze which made the heat more tolerable, but not by much.

Shelly came out after a few moments, wearing shorts and a white shirt. She hugged me from behind and kissed me on the back of the neck. She stepped beside me and I kissed her on the cheek, tossed an arm around her waist and gave her a hug as we listened to the morning.

Some kids were arguing at the house a few doors down, one of them accused the other of cheating while they played cops and robbers. The one was telling him he was dead, the other called him a name and told him he was stupid, besides using a couple of other words to define just what kind of stupid he was. Shelly looked at me and I shrugged, kids are kids, arguing with each other like they are gonna tear each other's heads off and the next walking arm in arm, best buddies.

As I stood there I kept thinking about the two Gates

boys and the more I thought about them the more I was convinced they were lying to me and the more convinced they weren't her brothers. Shelly poked an elbow in my ribs and I jumped, grunting and giving her a hurt look.

"What's going on in that mind of yours right now?" she asked as I looked at her, "I hope it's last night."

"Oh, I got that stored away for a rainy day, Kitten." I smiled at her to ease her mind, and to let her know she was special. "I was thinking about the Gates boys, their sister and the dead girl. Something isn't right, but what I haven't figured it out yet. Besides, I haven't told them about the girl yet."

"Smart move. Didn't you tell me their daddy had passed away?"

"Yeah, they said they had a disagreement and she left, could've been a fight over money." I peered across the street at the neighbors.

"Maybe." She followed my gaze. Across the street, Art Miller waved. His wife, sitting beside him, waved also, but just barely. Like us, they were out on the front porch enjoying the morning before it got hot. She leaned over and whispered something in his ear. He laughed and slapped his leg; she got up, pointed a finger at him, went back into the house, and slammed the screen door shut.

Art stood, ambled down the steps and crossed the street his pipe sat firm between his lips. Art was a big man. By big I mean three hundred pounds big. He wore overalls with the buttons unbuttoned on the sides and a white, sleeveless undershirt; his feet were clad in a pair of house slippers that slapped the pavement and concrete sidewalk with every step. His face showed his age, heavily lined and deeply tanned from all his years of working in the rail yard. His bluish-gray eyes had a permanent squint to them.

The only hair left on his head was along the sides with a few strays still on top. He kept the sides clipped short and what showed was a light gray color.

"Hello, Max, Shelly" he said taking the pipe out of his mouth and waving.

"Hey Art," I said as he climbed the steps, the wood screaming under his weight.

"How's your wife, Art?" Shelly asked grinning.

"Still troutin' the wages of sin you two are livin' in."

I grinned and sipped more coffee. Emma, Art's wife was a devout Bible Thumper. She had visited Shelly a couple of times and told her in no uncertain terms she was living in sin. Shelly had been nice and listened to her spout off. When she left, Shelly had called her Aunt Allie about it and Allie had just laughed and told her not to worry, Emma had had her say and she wouldn't bother her again. She hadn't, but poor Art had caught the brunt of it ever since.

"You two kids look as happy as clams." Art winked, Shelly blushed and went back inside. He laughed, turned, stepped down one step and parked his butt on the porch.

"Shelly's a good woman." He took the pipe from his mouth. "You love her?"

I parked beside him. "Yeah, I do," I sat my cup down and pulled a cigar from my shirt pocket.

"Good, that's all that counts. I have known her and her brother ever since they bought this house. Worked with him for a while on the railroad. He's the one you're going to have to convince you're good enough for his sister, may even have to fight him before it's over with." He cast a wary eye at me.

"Whatever it takes." I replied.

"Good man." Art struck a match and puffed on his pipe.

"Listen," I said after he had his pipe going, "Take a look at this and tell me if you have seen this girl around here."

I pulled the photo out of my shirt pocket and handed it to him. He looked at it for a long moment, puffed on his pipe and then handed it back.

"She looks familiar, especially her eyes. She may have been working in one of the diners up around the square," he said.

"Remember which one?" I asked him.

Art rubbed his chin and stared out into the street, his mind going back.

"Sorry Max," he said, "Like I said, I do remember her eyes though, prettiest blue eyes I've ever seen."

"Blue, huh? Thanks, Art, gives me something to go on."

"Arthur!"

Art shook his head. "The queen calls!" He laughed again as he hefted himself up from the porch then tottered across the street. He winced when she yelled again, then yelled back, "Don't get your panties in a bunch. I'm coming!"

Shelly came back out and sat down beside me. A cup of coffee in her hand, she shook her head as Art climbed the steps of his porch and went into the house.

"Hope you don't get like that when we get old and gray together," I said watching her out of the corner of my eye.

"No, I don't think so," she said giggling, "Hope you don't get fat like that either."

I stood, shook my head and grinned, handed her my cup, bent down and pecked her on the top of the head and started to leave. She stood, and set the cups down.

"We can do better than that," she said and hung a kiss on me, this one hotter than the air around us. When we broke, I glanced over across the street. The curtains in Art's living room were partly opened, and then dropped shut. I could hear Emma talking to Art, preaching how there wasn't any modesty in the younger generation anymore.

I glanced at Shelly. "You knew she was there didn't you?" She gave me a coy smirk.

My heart did a little dance, but I knew I had some

things to do, so I stood then gave her a little kiss. "Later, Kitten. Stay home today, I've got some footwork to do. No need for you to burn up in the office."

CHAPTER 5

There were a lot less people on the street than yesterday. The heat kept people at home in front of the fans when they didn't have anything better to do. As I passed the alley beside my office, I saw two winos, one leaning against the wall, drinking from a bottle, the other passed out, his head propped against a trashcan for a pillow. Both were dressed in a few layers of clothes, the one drinking wiped sweat from his face with his dirty shirt sleeve.

I could have called the cops and turned them in, vagrants not allowed, especially drunk ones, but with the heat and all, I figured they were better off. At least they were in the shade till the sun moved on and centered itself over the city, then they would mosey on unless a beat cop ran across them. Then *he* would mosey them along.

I unlocked the office door, and when I opened it a blast of heat rolled out and slapped me in the face. I took off my hat and stepped inside just long enough to grab a light jacket, and my rig that holds my .45, out of my locked cabinet and strapped it on. I tossed the jacket over my shoulder to hide the piece. Even though most people here in town know me, the sight of the artillery I carry still gets me looks from a few, but this piece has kept me alive many a time so I let them look.

Today was Thursday and I figured that was why so few people were wandering the streets. Tomorrow would be a little more hectic since it was payday and Saturday would be the most hectic, heat or no heat. Farmers from outside the city would come in and buy supplies, city folks who didn't have time to shop after getting off of work would hit the stores to see what bargains they could dicker the price down on. Then there was Saturday night: the young people would come in to go to the movies or to one of the dances I had seen advertised around town. Life in the city, you got to love it heat wave or no.

Oh, and Saturday night is also the night the army boys come in to party, about a hundred of them–security from the rail yard since the trains carrying military supplies passed through there. Those boys can get very wild, very loud and very ugly once they get juiced up. All someone has to do is say the wrong thing or they can do the wrong thing and the brawl is on.

That's the night Pat and his boys have their hands full, the M.P.s taking care of the solider boys and Pat and his men taking care of the county and city boys who want to kill the solider boys for making passes at their girlfriends; the solider boys just looking to toss off some steam from having to listen to hard-assed commanders run them around in the heat. Fun times all around.

I hopped a city bus and took it to the bus stop in front of the Colonial Hotel. A big banner advertised cool air in bold red letters, the first thing you saw when you got off the bus. As I stepped off, the doorman of the hotel ushered out a fellow dressed a little shabby and cussing up a storm. Guess he had been found snoozing in one of the corners inside, down the maintenance hallway.

The back entrance was easily jimmied from the outside

to give them access. Sometimes Mel, the night manager, leaves it open, whether it is on purpose or he just forgets, either way, the guy has a big heart and feels for the down trodden. He keeps it up he's gonna be one of the downtrodden himself. I shook my head and crossed the street to Cully's as the bum and the doorman cussed up a storm at each other.

Cully's was located on the corner of McDaniel and Jefferson, right across from the Veteran's Hall which had been built on a mound of dirt held in place by a concrete retaining wall. Someone once told me the small hill had some sort of historical meaning to it, they just couldn't remember what it was.

Cully's was a smaller place than Benny's, my normal lunch stop on Commercial Street but was set up about the same. Lunch counter and chrome based stools with red leather seats along the south wall and booths of red leather along the windows. There were very few people in the diner and with the way the heat was building outside it made me wonder. Cold or heat, Benny's is always full during the noon hour. Benny's food was claimed by all to be the best in town.

As I walked in, a couple of the customers eyed me and I nodded, knowing then why there were very few people in the diner. These guys looked more like they belonged behind bars than behind a table. Cully's fans churned the hot air in the diner but made it tolerable.

I sat down on a stool at the lunch counter. A waitress came over, chewing gum and holding an order pad in one hand, she reached for the pencil tucked in her bottled blonde hair. She leaned slightly over the counter, her cleavage pushed against the low cut uniform blouse. She looked me up and down; a big smile crossed her face.

"What'll ya have, sugar?" she said in a sultry voice, her eyes telling me what *she* would like to have.

I grinned and looked her in the eyes. "Cully around?"

She straightened, pouted her lips, and then giggled. "Hey Bert," she called over her shoulder. This guy wants to speak to Cully!"

Something akin to a gorilla stepped out of the doorway. Bert was all muscle. His arms were as big as tree limbs and his chest as broad as a barn. He had no neck, his head just sitting on his shoulders. His face was the face of a fighter, his nose flattened, his right ear shaped like a cauliflower and his lips looked like they were permanently fattened.

He came out of the kitchen wiping his hands on a greasy rag and then stuck his hand out. I took it and his grip was like a vice. Lucky he didn't clasp my hand too long.

"Cully's the past owner's name. I bought the place from him. Just ain't never changed it. Bert Mills is the name."

"Max Black."

"I've heard of you." He leaned on the counter with both hands, "What can I do for you, Mr. Black?"

"How long you owned this place?"

"'Bout a year. The old guy's wife was gonna close it down. I picked it up for a song. Always wanted a business."

I glanced around, then looked straight at him. "It doesn't look like business is too good."

"It's the heat," Bert eyed me back. The blonde was standing behind him making eyes at me, and not the sexy kind. I reached in my jacket pocket with one hand, took out a cigar and lipped it, with my other hand I tossed the photo on the counter.

"You ever have this girl work here?" I asked striking a match and lighting the cigar.

He picked it up and scanned it close, his eyes narrowed a second. Then he shook his head. "Don't remember her." He laid the image on the counter. "Might have worked here when the original owner had it."

"Is he still around?" I asked.

"Nope," he said jerking his thumb to the west wall. A photo of a man dressed in clothes dating back to the early thirties hung on the wall. An 'In Memory Of' plaque hung beneath it.

"Any idea where she might be working?" I took the picture back and slid it in my pocket.

"Nope."

I got the impression that if I asked anymore questions things might get nasty, so I smiled, said thanks and exited the joint. As I walked to the door and out I watched out of the corner of my eye. As I flicked ash from the cigar, Bert picked up a phone from under the counter and talked to the operator. I walked back to the bus stop and stood, the sun beating down and the heat waves shimmering.

Five minutes passed and a car pulled up to Bert's. A fellow dressed in a suit crawled out and went inside. He and Bert talked for a few minutes, then he left. Bert followed and the two of them looked across the street. I had moved into the shadows of the Colonial's front steps, just enough to be out of sight.

They talked for a few more minutes then he crawled into the car. Bert pointed a finger at him and the man gave him a one finger salute as they pulled away. Bert cursed and gave them the Italian high sign as he stomped back into the diner.

I was hoping they would turn around and come back toward me but they didn't so I kept watch on the diner from my hiding place. Bert was on the phone again, this time using his arms to accent what he was saying. What few customers he had kept staring at him. He slammed the receiver down and stomped back into the kitchen.

The bus pulled up and cut off my view. As I stepped out then boarded, I shoved my token in the slot and slid into a seat. The bleached blonde argued with Bert in the serving window of the kitchen for all to see. I laughed and leaned back in the seat. The bus went down one block then turned onto Market Street where Pat and his detectives made their home.

CHAPTER 6

The Station, as it has always been called, is a red brick, two story building located on Market Street and seems to be the first building in the city that had a basement. Said basement houses the holding cells. The outsides were in pretty good shape after all these years but it was the insides that had taken a beating over the years. I mean, repairs were made regularly when the money was available, but since the war, things had gotten a little run down, mostly in the basement where the holding cells were.

A few cells seeped water and the walls were littered with graffiti. Of course the bad guys didn't mind, hell, it was paradise compared to the county cells. Pat was sitting at his desk, a fan just blowing the hot air in the room on him. His office was at the south end of the Detective's Squad room on the second floor, a small cubical, six feet by eight feet cluttered with papers and file folders piled on his desk. A chair sat on the right side of his desk, a small couch along the wall faced his desk. Cigarette smoke filled the room along with the faint smell of sweat and gun oil.

Pat is a big, red headed Irish lug. The guy is all cop. He goes by the book, but doesn't go by it completely when things get dicey, stretching the rules to sometimes breaking. I explained the trace I was working on to him, then handed him the picture. He stared at it for a few seconds, then handed it back then yelled for Carl Maxwell. Carl came in and I handed him the picture. He scanned it close for a few minutes and handed it back with a head shake.

Carl was the only vice cop they had left. His other cronies, both of them, had been recruited into the European Theater to fight Hitler. Carl tried to join but was turned down. A bout with pneumonia when he was young had damaged his lungs.

"Her name is Becky Gates," I said while he was still looking at the picture.

"She looks familiar." He shrugged "Can't place her right now, though."

"Thanks Carl," Pat said.

Carl saluted and went back to his desk, picked up a couple of things and left. He was a busy guy. Pat had tried to get stand-ins for his partners, but the city council said no. So when he got enough evidence for a bust, he used Pat's patrol officers. I described the guy Bert had talked to.

Pat nodded and leaned back in his chair. "The guy you described sounds like one of Ava's boys"

I nodded. Ava Peasant's house was on the south side of town just outside the city limits in the county's jurisdiction, so she was pretty much left alone. Why you might ask? Well, Sheriff Dunn visits once in a while, so there you have it. It's a big Victorian place she had bought a few years back, refurbished and opened for business.

"I wonder if she knows anything." I rubbed my chin.

"No doubt you're going to go see her and find out," Pat said, "Just remember, go unarmed, you know how she feels about guns."

I grinned. I knew of that certain incident. It involved a couple of hoods from St. Louis who had come down here and tried to take over her business. They knew of her aversion to firearms and came in loaded for bear. They left with their tails between their legs. She might hate guns, but she sure wasn't past letting her boys use them.

"Better not let Shelly find out you've gone there," Pat said chuckling, "Remember what happened the last time."

I nodded and waved goodbye as I walked out of his office. The last time I had trailed a bail jumper to Ava's house, the guy was hiding out in his girlfriend's room. Ava had given him up the minute I appeared and after a rousing fist fight. I knocked him out and turned him over to the police who said I smelled like a French whore house. The girlfriend had more bottles of perfume than any woman has a right to own.

Shelly razzed me about it for a month, and so did Pat, but I endured all except for the nickname, Malodorous Max. That took a while to live down, if you know what I mean.

CHAPTER 7

I decided to see Ava the next day, which gave me a little time to slum around and see if any of my other contacts recognized Becky Gates. It was the same as Art and the others told me. She looked familiar but nobody could place her. Maybe I would have more luck with Ava.

Ava's house looked like any other in the city, white with brown shutters, a porch that ran the length of the front and around the side. The only things different than any other houses close were the wrought iron chairs and tables with glass tops that sat on the porch, red velvet cushions on the chairs, the glass tops of the tables etched with designs.

It was a little after ten in the morning when I knocked on the door. After a few minutes a little blonde cutie opened it.

"Well, it's a little early for customers," She lifted a leg out of her silk robe, and with a more than sexy move, rubbed it up and down the edge of the door. "But...."

She was a cutie alright, with a body that spelled all woman. Probably just a little over five feet tall, she had on a thin robe, the shoulders draped around her arms and the fabric so sheer I could see the red garters that held up her hose.

She was well endowed, the cleavage deep and her girls threatening to spill out of the teddy she had on. Her hair was cut in a pageboy, the ends curled slightly under and her bangs spilling down to her eyebrows. Her eyes were an emerald green and flashed mischief when she spoke.

"Sorry doll, I came to see Ava."

Her lips pushed out in a pout. "Rats." She opened the door to let me in.

I didn't even get out of the entryway before a big fellow appeared. He looked me over and grunted. He was big and ugly and nothing to be fooled with unless armed with a trench gun to equal the odds.

"What's your business here," he growled.

"I would like to speak to Miss Peasant."

"Nobody goes in until searched," he growled again, "You packin'?"

I lifted my jacket open wide. He grunted and nodded.

"What's under the hat?"

"My hair."

"Smart ass, take it off."

I did and he looked the hat over, then handed it to the girl. "Hold this, Elsa."

"Pull your pant legs up."

"Why, you got a thing for hairy ankles?"

The girl giggled and he shot her a look. "Raise em', wise ass," He stepped forward a bit.

I did what he asked and he stepped back. I started to take my hat back and he stopped me.

"You can pick it up when you leave," he said, taking it from Elsa.

She smiled and motioned for me to follow. She stopped in the main room and told me to have a seat; she would tell Ava I was here. I plopped on a beige sofa and looked around. I had been in a few pleasure houses in my time but none of then looked like this, none of them looked this normal. There were no red velvet curtains framing the windows, no red lamp shades or naughty pictures on the walls. Everything was in good taste, furnished as if a regular family lived there. The floor was covered by expensive, Persian rugs; the curtains were sheer fabric of pale blue, dark blue ones hanging over them all tied back with tasseled ties of a darker blue color.

The lamps were Victorian, hand painted with scenes of water falls and lakes, the shades made of silk and trimmed with smaller tassels around the bottoms. Yep, not your typical house of ill repute. I was about to check out one of those old time post card viewers when Ava walked in.

Tall and red headed, she was a beautiful woman. She wore a silk robe of pale blue belted tight around her waist with a dark blue leather belt. Her shoes were flats of the same color and when she walked, her legs came out of the front of the robe long and silky. She was well endowed, the silk robe accenting her girls. I stood and took her hand.

"Mr. Black," she said sitting down on the sofa beside me. Her robe fell away from those sexy legs. "I hope my man didn't offend you with our precautions?"

"Nope, I can understand why you have those precautions in place."

She smiled and nodded. "Now, what do you wish to talk to me about?"

I pulled the picture out of my shirt pocket and showed it to her. She took it and for a moment, her eyes widened.

"Her name is Becky Gates." I said watching her close, "Her brothers have hired me to find her."

"I see."

"Do you know her?"

Ava smiled and shook her head. "No, sorry I don't."

"Well, have you ever..."

She stood suddenly, the blonde girl appeared just as quickly beside me.

"No, Mr. Black." Her voice was cold when she handed me back the picture, "I have never seen, nor know, nor have had this girl working here. Now, if you will follow Elsa she will escort you to the front door."

And that was that. Now, normally I would of grabbed her by the arm and slammed her pretty ass back down on the couch and asked her the question again, but I had a feeling big and ugly was close by, ready to stomp someone if they made trouble. I watched her waltz away as Elsa took me by the arm and waltzed me to the door, trying every trick she knew to keep my attention focused on her. The gorilla was standing at the door with my hat. I took it as he opened the door. Elsa wished me a goodbye and come again, and the door slammed shut as I walked out to my car, crawled in and fired it up.

Something bugged me, something I had seen while Elsa was walking me to the door. Something I caught out of the corner of my eye while she kept my eyes on her. Dames will do that you know, especially if they're trying to hide something. Elsa was doing a hell of a job of it, that *something* kept me occupied while I drove back to the office and then some.

CHAPTER 8

The next morning Shelly had come in to do some catch up paper work before the heat kicked into high gear. She opened bills and filed papers she had finished a few days before. She also told me the next time I sat at her desk to be sure and clean the dirt from my number nines off of it and bring my ashtray out there, not use her candy dish for an ashtray. Dames, ya gotta love em'.

As all this was going on I was in my office thinking. My fan tossed hot air at me as I tried to remember what I had seen. It was right on the edge of my mental tongue, hiding and teasing me, laughing its ass off each time I almost nabbed it before it slipped away.

I heard the door open and voices came back to me, Orville and Chet's voices. Then Shelly came into my office, her face red.

"The Gates brothers are here to see you," she said, then stepped to the door and told them to come in. They entered and as she passed Chet she jumped. Chet grinned at her and Shelly gave him a dirty look as she exited.

"That is some fine secretary you got there Mr. Black,"

Chet said, winking, "A real fine filly."

"Yeah and you do that again and you might lose a hand." I leaned forward. "She might look good, but she is meaner than hell when it comes to other men making passes at her, especially since she is taken."

I let that sink in for a moment and then Chet's face went red.

"She is spoken for, Mr. Black?" he said in a strained voice.

"That's what I said, bub," I answered him in a low growl. Chet stuttered he was sorry and he would surely apologize to the lady when he left. I nodded and told them I hadn't found anything yet. Orville shook his head.

"We went to where our cousins used to call home way out north on Avenue Road," he said, "Place is no longer there. Burned up in a fire couple of years back."

"That's too bad," I said nodding.

"Well, we just came back to tell you we will be leaving shortly, business to tend to up St. Louie way. We would appreciate it if you would continue to see if you can find Becky," he said.

"Yeah," I replied and looked at the both of them. The gnawing came back and nipped at the edges of my mind when they said her name, but for some reason, it wouldn't gnaw through.

Orville reached into his coat and took out another envelope, tossed it on the desk without the ritual straightening. I picked it up and there was more money in it, a lot more. There was also an address of a hotel where they would be staying in St. Louis.

"That should hold you for a while," he said standing, "We'll be here at the Missouri a couple more days and then we'll be gone."

"Yeah, more than a while," I said, then stood and shook their hands. They went out the door and I stepped beside it and listened as Chet stuttered an apology to

Shelly. I went back to my desk. Shelly came in after a few minutes and I handed her the envelope.

"Are you ok?" I asked her.

"I am now," she said thumbing through the money. "At least the bills will get paid and there will be some left over."

As she turned to leave I pinched her left butt cheek and she squealed.

"Only I get to do that," I said with a smile.

She flashed a seductive smile my way and pushed her hip out toward me. I made a move to get up and rush her. She giggled and shot out the door. The sound of someone colliding with Shelly made her yelp. I started to stand, but when I heard Al's voice I settled back into my chair.

"Oh Al, I'm so sorry," I heard Shelly say.

"It's ok Shell." He laughed.

"Max," Shelly yelled.

"Come on in Al." I yelled back.

Al came in and Shelly started to shut the door, but I waved her off.

"So this is how you conduct business when things get slow," Al said loud enough for Shelly to hear out where she sat. She groaned and started pounding on the typewriter.

"Gotta admit it keeps things from getting boring," I said with a chuckle.

"So, how is the trace case coming?"

"Nothing so far, why?"

"Well, Jax was at the shop yesterday and said he saw a couple of guys last night you might want to know about.

"Any indication what it was about?"

"Nope, just said to let you know when I saw you. Figured I'd better check and see if you were in."

"Thanks Al, I'll go see him this afternoon."

"You're welcome," Al stood and before he exited my office he spoke to Shelly. Something thumped the wall as he laughed and zipped out the door, Shelly muttered something about men.

***

Jax Jazz occupied a renovated warehouse on McDaniel Street. Once a PI like me, Jax ran into some trouble, got his gun permit pulled with no opportunity of getting it back and almost landed his ass in the state pen. He took what money he had left, and opened the club. It's a nice place. The interior brick walls made great background for posters of famous Jazz artists and bands. A big mahogany bar ran the length of the east wall. Jax told me it had come from a St. Louis place that had been one of Capone's joints. The speakeasy had been raided by competitors. A tommy gun during a raid left a row of bullet holes in the front of the bar. Jax had left them. Figured it gave the bar class, something to tell the patrons about.

About every kind of whiskey anyone could want lined glass shelves in front of a mirror that ran the full length of the wall. The club's tables and chairs were imported and not the usual four legs and straight backs. Jax' tables had round tops with a center pedestal that flared out into four feet. Jax told me one time he had seen the same tables in a Chicago club during Prohibition days and he knew the man who owned them. He got them for a song when the man got religion and declared he would never sell the demon rum again. Now he sold salvation and packed the house each night.

Wrought iron chairs at least three feet tall with leather seats flanked the tables. The chairs Jax made high enough for a drunk to know when he fell onto the floor that it was time to leave. The tables and chairs edged a dance floor of polished walnut and a bandstand.

Jax Jazz Club was a high spot in town. Friday and Saturday nights the club hopped with people there for the Jazz, the expensive whiskey—if they had the money, and sometimes things get a little rowdy. That was where Milt came in. Milt, a mountain of a Black man, hailed from Mississippi. When Milt tossed you out you knew it.

It was about six o'clock when I got there and already the sounds of laughter and clinking glasses filled the air.

The kid at the door was a big teddy bear by the name of Jimmy. Not too much in the smarts department, but good at spotting a guy with a gun. I've seen him look a guy over while shaking his hand and before the guy knew it, he hugged the wall and Jimmy had frisked him.

When I walked up to Jimmy he grinned and pumped my hand till I thought it was gonna fall off.

"Long time no see," Jimmy said, "How's that lovely, leggy woman of yours doing?"

"She's fine Jimmy." I lifted my coat and showed him my piece. He made a noise with his mouth and shook his head.

"No need pal" He pulled me through the door way. He nodded to one of the other door guys who nodded back and stepped in front of the couple that tried to follow us in. The guy didn't complain too much because this door guy was almost as big as Milt but a little uglier. Jimmy took me right to Jax's office, knocked, then opened the door and motioned me in.

Jax Jackson was a short man, about 5'4" with tailored suits, manicured nails and coal black hair cut in the latest style. Under his coat a .45 rests, for self-defense, the bulge not even noticeable even when he buttoned up. He stood and we shook hands. Jax offered me a Havana which I took and placed in my jacket pocket for later.

"Sit down, Max." He motioned to a chair. "Guess Al finally found you."

"Uh-huh."

"Word is out you're working a trace case, looking for a Becky Gates?"

"I am."

"And you're still looking because you don't believe the girl that was found in the river was her?"

"Yeah, something like that."

Jax reached in his desk and pulled out a file folder, opened it and laid it in front of me.

"Are these the two that hired you?"

I looked at the picture and cursed under my breath.

"Read the caption under the picture."

I read it and let out a low whistle. Both Orville and Chet had been killed in a distillery blast last year. A newspaper clipping showed a portion of the building they were working in completely demolished. They had lied to me. Remember what I said about liars?

"Those two that hired you are a couple of Holton's men," Jax said. "They were in here a couple of nights ago. Milt recognized them. Now answer me this, why would Holton send two of his goons down if he thought this Gates girl was dead?"

"He wouldn't, so what does Holton want with her, if she can be found?" I asked, and tossed the folder back on his desk.

"Well, I did a little checking and word has it that Holton is trying to buy the distillery. He contacted the two of them once and they told him to bug off. He tried a few scare tactics and they, being the good old boys they were, put his boys on the run. Rumor was that Holton had something to do with the blast, but that wasn't the case here. The accident was an accident. A faulty boiler built up pressure and while the two of them was trying to shut it down, it popped."

"So when Holton went to their lawyer and tried to buy what was left of the place, the lawyer told him there was a sister still alive. He didn't know where, but she would have to be the one to authorize the sale of the distillery since she was now the owner."

"So Holton sends two of his goons to hire someone to

find her," I said.

Jax nodded.

"Mind if I hang onto this?" I picked up the folder again.

"Be my guest. Hope I've helped."

"More than you know buddy. More than you know."

CHAPTER 9

The Missouri is one of the more reasonable hotels here in town, not quite as respectable as the Kentwood or the Colonial, but the rates are affordable, the rooms nice, just not as fancy. The Missouri used to cater to the railroad people when the tracks were being built and still do, but not as much as they did. The rates fit a lot of people's budgets since money was as tight as the bark of a tree since the war started.

Two bucks a day or five dollars a week was the going rate right now, which ain't bad considering the Colonial charges four to five bucks a day and the weekly rates are eight.

In the lobby there is a big mahogany desk for check in and a cigar stand to the left of the entrance to the dining room. Then there's the dining room where a fellow can get a rib-eye steak if he can afford it, or the local favorite, deep fried catfish with all the trimmings. There have been a lot of famous people stay here over the years, and a lot of unsavory people, too. Two of them occupied one of the rooms now.

I crossed to the desk and cleared my throat to get the skinny desk guy's attention. When that didn't work, I slammed my hand down on the bell. He turned and gave me the eye.

"May I help you Mr. Black?"

His voice was sarcastic. I recognized him from a job I worked before, one that almost cost him his job and a prison term. He looked like a weasel in a second hand suit. I still say he was guilty, but they just couldn't get enough evidence on him to ship him away.

"Yeah, the Gates brothers still bunked here?" I watched him look me up and down like I was some kind of nasty on his shoe and then checked the book.

"Why yes, yes they are, shall I announce you?" he said in a sarcastic tone and reached for the phone. I shook my head and grinned at him.

"Nope, just tell me what room they are in and I'll do that myself," I forced a smile.

He gave a grunt and told me the room number, which I already knew but wanted to see if he gave me the right one. The minute I started up the stairs he picked up the phone and told the switchboard operator to connect him.

The room, 204, was right in the middle of the hall. I stepped up to the door. I could hear feet scuffling inside. I pounded on the door. Chet opened it and glared at me.

"Max." His glare turned into surprise.

"Hey Chet, is your brother around?" I leaned in to see who was inside. Chet closed the door a little to block my view.

"No, no, he went downtown to see if he could drum up some business before we left. Always thinking of new business that brother of mine," he said with a nervous chuckle. His eyes darted to his right ever so often, his face covered in a thin sheen of sweat.

"Well, tell him I stopped by to give him this." I handed him a manila envelope.

"Ok. Did you find out something?" He looked from me to the envelope.

"Brother, you don't know the half of it!"

"Oh, good, good. Anything else?"

I heard a giggle from the other side of the door. "No, just that." I turned and walked away. The door closed and I could hear the faint sound of a woman laughing. I grinned and took the stairs back down to the lobby, saluted the desk clerk and left the building. I pulled the Havana Jax gave me from my jacket pocket and lit up. When they got a load of what was inside of the package, they'd come find me.

I stopped off at Pat's office and told him what Jax had told me, and what I had done. He let out a low whistle and shook his head.

"Dragging the rats out of the wood pile now, are we?"

"Hey, I don't like to be lied too, especially by hoods looking to strong arm someone!"

"Someone who is either dead or who hasn't been found?"

"Yeah, that's right. Besides, my gut tells me that the girl from the river isn't Becky."

"Your gut?"

Yeah, my gut," I growled at him.

I stood and walked to his door, then back again. The little something I'd seen at Ava's still tormented me.

"Something besides this is bugging you," Pat said. "What is it?"

I let out a sigh and shook my head.

"This and that something I got a glimpse of at Ava's, I mean this pisses me off but the other keeps trying to gnaw its way into my brain and it is driving me crazy."

"Well, don't let it make you go psycho," Pat said.

I gave him the eye and he shrugged. A couple of years back I had been on a case where a child had been abducted. I found her in an oil drum, her throat slit. I hunted the guy down who had done it and gave him no quarter when he came at me with a machete; two in the legs, two in the arms and two on either side of his heart. Then I stood over him and blew his balls off and was about to put one between his eyes when Pat and his boys showed up and stopped me. I guess I did go a little overboard but when I saw what he had done to that child....

"Sorry Pat," I tossed the memory to the back of my mind, "I just wish I hadn't been so distracted by the cutie that led me out."

"Yeah, they can do that," he answered.

"Wonder if the Gates' are sweating after seeing what I left them?" I felt a big smirk spread over my face.

"Oh, I suspect they are."

I stood, told him I would see him later and was out the door. The gnawing continued as I grabbed a cab and headed to Shelly's to cool down for the rest of the evening.

CHAPTER 10

There was a car in Shelly's drive when we crossed the railroad tracks. I told the driver to stop, dug the money out, paid him, then walked the rest of the way up to the house. There was a light on in the kitchen but all the rest of the house was dark. I slid up to the window that opened above the sink, listened for a moment and heard Orville curse.

"Damn it! I told the boss this wouldn't work. This shamus isn't some local yokel."

"Yeah." Chet scratched his head. "Think he might be mad?"

"Oh shut the hell up you moron, of course he will be mad! But we got insurance to keep him from getting too mad."

Then I heard Shelly's voice. Even in this heat, coldness crept up my spine along with a flash of anger as I pulled out my .45. I jacked back the hammer slowly to keep the click from being heard.

"Oh, my man will be mad, all right. You bastards are going to be sorry for using me. Max will see to that!"

Yeah, the both of them were gonna find out just how

mad in a few minutes. I had to get Shelly out of there.

A chair scrape on the floor, and footsteps walked to the sink. Water ran and a glass clinked against the faucet. I leaned back. Chet was getting a drink. A thought ran through my head, but if it went wrong, things could get pretty bad in a hurry. He was about to set the glass in the sink when I tapped the side of the house with the muzzle of my .45.

I counted on Chet being as dumb as he looked, and he was. He leaned halfway out the window, and I brought the pistol up hard on the side of his head. The sight on the muzzle of my .45 cut a slash on his cheek as he jerked his head to the side.

He cursed and grabbed my wrist. His other hand struggled under his coat and came out with a snub-nosed .38. I twisted loose from his hand and pointed the .45 at his face. Chet jerked his head to the side again as I fired. The slug grazed his head and knocked him out. I grabbed him with both hands and jerked him out the window.

As he hit the ground, I made a dash toward the back door of the house. I hoped the sudden attack on Chet would rattle Orville enough for me to get to him. But Orville came out the back door with Shelly in tow as I reached the corner of the house.

The girl fought him, kicking at his shins as he tried to land a blow on her head. I stopped at the corner and stepped back. When he reached the corner of the house, I grabbed Shelly by the arm and pulled her out of his grasp. Orville cussed and staggered back. His pistol came up but I didn't give him time to fire, just unloaded three in his chest up close. He dropped like rock.

Shelly ran past me, yelling. She kicked the recovering Chet in the head as he tried to get up. He went out again with a grunt.

"Bastard!" she hissed between her teeth and kicked him again. She was gonna give him another one but I stopped her.

"Easy Kitten, we need him alive."

"Sum bitch felt me up!"

She landed one last kick before I could stop her. I pulled her back and held onto her till she stopped shaking, then I kissed her and held her some more. Art came running around the side of the house, skidded to a halt, and looked from Chet to Orville to me. He had a shotgun gripped in both hands.

"Call the Station," I said. He nodded and took off again. Twenty minutes later, Pat came around the house and looked down at Chet who started to come round again.

"One alive, one dead," I jerked my thumb over my shoulder.

Pat walked over to Orville. He shook his head as he came back to Shelly. "You ok?"

She nodded and I took her in the house while Pat's boys cuffed Chet and hauled him away. Orville would have to wait for the coroner.

CHAPTER 11

I convinced Pat to let Shelly stay with me for the rest of the night. I told him I would bring her down the Station in the morning to make a statement. He said okay then asked why Chet wasn't dead. I shrugged and told him Chet was just lucky, another inch and he would have joined Orville in hell. He grunted and walked away.

"They came about six o'clock and asked if you were here," she said, wiping her eyes. "I told them no and they told me they needed to talk to you and asked when you would be back. I told them I didn't know when you would be back and they asked if they could wait. I told them no again and that was when Orville pulled his gun and they forced their way in. I ran and tried to get to the back door. That...that one who calls himself Chet ran after me and caught me before I could get out. He pawed me all over, Max. And he laughed while he did it!"

She started to cry again so I held her and let her cry. Tomorrow, after the questions were done, I was gonna break all Chet's fingers, one at a time.

***

"His name is Gino Case, the dead one is Wiley Burns. They are out of St. Louis. Enforcers, the FBI says. Part of Holton's crew," Pat handed me the information the feds had sent down. "These two were very bad boys with long rap sheets filled with arrests, but no convictions."

"You question Che... I mean Gino yet?" I asked.

"Yeah, but he doesn't seem afraid of me. He told me to get him a lawyer, but when I mentioned the Feds were on their way, he got bug eyed and said he definitely wanted a lawyer."

"The Feds?" I looked at him.

"Yeah, when I called them about these guys, they said they would contact their agent here in the Federal Building." He curled his lip. "I don't like it any better than you, Max."

"Well, maybe we should try one more time before the home town Fed gets here?" I hoped he'd agree.

He nodded and we went to the stairs, then down to the cells. Pat told the jailer on duty to go get some coffee. He handed Pat the keys, stood up from the desk, nodded, and left in a little too much of a hurry.

He was someone I'd never seen before, and I got suspicious. When I looked at Pat, I knew he was, too. "I thought the city wasn't hiring any new guys." Reality hit and we made a run for the cell. Pat fumbled with the keys as we ran, and cussed a blue streak 'til he got the cell unlocked.

Gino had a piece of rope tied around his neck, the other end looped over a pipe running along the ceiling. His body had been hauled up. Gino's hands had been tied behind him with another piece of rope, and a piece of a rag shoved into his mouth to muzzle him. His legs had been broken to keep him from holding himself up since the ceiling was low.

Gino had been roughed up good this time. Barely conscious and bleeding, his face had a bluish cast to it. Pat opened his pocket knife and cut the rope while I held him. I eased him onto the floor the best I could without causing him more pain. I took his pulse. It was weak but there. Pat ran upstairs and yelled for someone to call an ambulance. Two detectives came back down with him.

The man was coming around when the ambulance got there. They hauled him to City Hospital with instructions to not let anyone but police or hospital personnel in his room.

"Where is the man that was on duty tonight, what was his name?" Pat growled.

One of the detectives frowned. "It was supposed to be Duffy, but he's home sick. Monroe was supposed to take his place."

"That wasn't Monroe that gave me the keys." Pat ran his fingers through his hair, then looked at the two men. "Find the imposter, and find out what happened to Monroe."

Then he looked at me. "Holton must be cleaning up loose ends, silencing anyone who had contact with his boys. You best get over to Shelly's, just to be on the safe side."

I nodded and made tracks up the stairs and out the door to my car. Pat was right. Someone was cleaning up loose ends and anything that had been connected with it. Was it Holton? I had my doubts but, just to be on the safe side, I jumped in the car and tore out for Shelly's.

***

I slammed through the door. "Shelly?" She ran to me from the kitchen. I took her in my arms and hugged her tight. "Get some things together, you're going to move for a few days." I saw panic on her face.

"Max, what's wrong?"

I told her about Chet being Gino and her eyes got big. That's when a man stepped into the kitchen doorway.

"So, what's going down?"

He had half of sandwich in his hand. Who the hell was this guy? Shelly must have seen the question forming on my lips.

"Max, this is Jack, my brother. Why do I need to move?"

I had to be straight with her. "Those two guys were a couple of Holton's goons. He may be cleaning up loose ends, since I found out about why he was trying to find Becky." I released her from my embrace. Now get some clothes together and–"

"Whoa, hoss," Jack tossed the sandwich in his hand on a table. "Are you sure about this?"

"Look, sonny boy," I hissed, "My gut tells me that–"

We all three heard the car tires screech to a stop outside. I grabbed Shelly, pulled her to the floor, and braced myself on top of her. Jack dropped right behind us as the bull moan of a Thompson riddled the house with lead. I drew my .45 and cocked it. Jack looked at me, his eyes wide as the slugs tore up the walls and anything else in their path. Suddenly the noise stopped. The only sound was that of glass falling.

Footsteps sounded on the front porch. Then the door slammed open. Jack nodded and I waited till the footsteps were closer. I wouldn't move until the last minute.

I heard the bolt slam back on the Thompson again, and I rolled over and put one between the hood's eyes. He fell like a stone, and Jack grabbed the Thompson. We both came up off the floor. Jack fingered the trigger in short bursts while I pumped shots at the other two that were trying to back out of the doorway. They danced as we played their death song. The driver of the car hauled ass out of there before we could get out the door.

"Are they gone?" Shelly's voice was small.

"Yeah, Kitten, for now."

She came to me and I hugged her. "Now hurry and grab some things so we can get outta here." She took off toward the bedroom.

Jack settled the Thompson on his hip. He looked at the scene in front of us and grimaced. "Shelly was right, shoot first, ask questions later."

"My motto," I stated. "Of course we should have left one of them alive to ask questions to."

"Yeah, I guess we should of."

I walked over to where the Tommy gun man lay, hooked my foot under his body and turned him over on his back. I bent and searched him. He was clean, not even a piece of lint in his pockets.

"A hit squad." I stood. "No ID on them if they get whacked, but that doesn't mean they're not in the system. Hey, thanks for the help." I held out my hand and Jack took it.

"And thanks for taking care of my sister. She was right when she told me about how you were when it came to the bad guys. I guess you'll do, buddy."

Shelly came out of the bedroom with a stuffed suitcase. "I told you!" Sirens filled the hot air.

CHAPTER 12

Agent Tad Trent showed up with Pat, and asked the usual questions. Trent was the typical FBI man, tall, muscular and all business. He wandered around and looked over the stiffs we had produced. His square jawed face remained blank during his inspection. Pat looked at me and shook his head. I got his meaning. If the Feds took over, Pat would be taking orders from them and I would be out unless Pat could convince them otherwise.

"They are low grade enforcers," Trent said. He watched the coroner do his thing. "Pat briefed me on how all this started. We've been watching things here for a while."

"Watching things for a while? How long is a while?" I asked.

"Ever since the distillery explosion. We thought maybe it was Holton's doings, but it actually was an accident."

I didn't think it made sense. "Yeah, but why take *us* out for finding out two of his boys screwed up."

"Don't know." Trent glanced my way. "Any luck with the girl?"

"Which one?" I asked.

"Is there more than the Gates girl?" Trent looked at Pat.

"A girl turned up in the James River," I tried to cover Pat before he could say anything. "She may or may not be the Gates girl."

Pat shrugged. "We got a print and sent it off. It hasn't come back yet, so we don't know."

Trent nodded. "Maybe I can help speed that up."

I grunted and shook my head. Trent eyed me.

"Something on your mind?" He turned toward me.

"I don't think the dead girl is Gates," I stared him in the eyes.

"And how do you figure that?"

"I just do."

"Okay, but just in case, you don't mind if I hurry up the print?"

"Knock yourself out," I didn't back down.

Pat gave me a warning glance, then shifted his gaze to Trent. "What now?"

Trent pointed to me. "We work together. I hear Max has some good information sources. With my and his contacts, we should be able to wrap this up pretty quick."

Trent grinned and walked over to where the coroner worked. Pat made arrangements for Shelly's and Jack's hideaway.

Shelly wandered around the house, not touching anything but looking and shaking her head. All her memories in this room were shot to hell. Pictures, small figurines and other knick knacks lay shattered by the hoods' bullets.

She wiped her eyes and picked up a small china angel. One wing had broken off and there was a chip in the hem of the gown. "Aaron gave me this." She studied it.

One of the lab boys started to protest but Pat cut him

off with a nasty glance. He shrugged and went back to his business. I walked up beside her and hugged her close. A few tears rolled down her cheeks as she looked up at me.

"Can I..." she started to say.

I looked at Pat who nodded slightly and stepped in front of the lab boy who worked close. I took it from her hands and shoved it in my coat pocket.

"Thanks," she mouthed as I led her toward the door and out of the carnage.

I took Shelly and Jack to Al's in the middle of the night so as to keep the people who wanted to do us harm from finding us. Al lives in a small house just inside the city limits on South Street. When I called him he said it would be a little cramped, but they would manage.

Pat assigned one of his detectives to stand guard, briefing him on what he wanted him to do once we got to Al's. Trent went to the Federal Building to see if he could get a line on who these boys were and who they were working for, and to get a line on the dead girl's print.

As I drove Shelly and Jack to Al's, I tried again to get the thing tormenting my mind to come forward and show itself. It laughed at me each time. Shelly and Jack were in the back. They talked about the war and what he had been through.

Jack is Shelly's twin brother, which put him at 28 years old. His face has a rugged and outdoorsy look, his chin square with a dimple in the center of it. He has the same color eyes as Shelly, and he has her temper or vice versa. The army had made a lean, mean solider out of him, and it showed when we took out the hoods.

As we drove to Al's, Jack told us he had been with the 101st when they parachuted into Normandy just before the big offensive started. His squad had encountered some of the worst fighting during the wee hours of the morning before D-Day.

"A Lot of my buddies are in the ground over there. I

should have been, but my friend, Stan…," he paused and swallowed, his voice breaking.

"We were moving through the trenches, knocking out .88s before the landings started. The Germans tried to cut us down, but we moved too fast. We got to them before they had time to do anything. Four of us were stuffing C-2 into the muzzle of a .88 when this Nazi came screaming at us. He had a potato masher in his hand, and Kelly, our squad leader, cut him down with a Thompson. But when he fell, the Nazi pulled the pin on the masher and dropped it right in front of me. Stan grabbed me from behind and whirled me around. The blast a split second later. He died shortly after that."

We rode in silence for a while. Shelly held Jack's hand and wiped a tear away from her face every so often. Me, I wondered if the kid would ever be the same after what he had seen. I mean, back after the boys came back from WWI, some of them had dealt with it with drink and some with drugs. The ones dealing with it with drugs had been addicted to them while in the hospital, and when they came home that addiction ruled them.

My dad was one of the drinkers. He'd get wild assed drunk and tear the place we lived in apart. My mom and I ducked out and went to her sister's, where, if pops showed up, my uncle either talked him down or knocked the crap out of him and left him on the back porch draped over the woodpile to sleep it off. Mom and I then went back home.

Pops died from the booze. His liver gave up the ghost when he was fifty eight years old. Not a nice death, either. Jack's voice jerked me back to the present. His words hold an edge as he spoke.

"I was sent home to help sell war bonds," Jack grunted. "They called us heroes for knocking out the guns the way we did and we saved lives when the troops landed on the beaches. Said they needed us to promote the war effort. The real heroes are still there, wading in the mud and blood to keep the Nazis from taking over."

He looked at me in the rear view, and I nodded. He wanted to be back there with his buddies, taking ground and pushing the enemy back. But he was also a solider, and he had his orders, no matter what they were, and he followed orders.

Al and Allie live right on the edge of town, on a small five acre tract. The nearest neighbor lived almost a quarter of a mile away. But that was changing; a few new houses were going up in between Al and his neighbors—ranch style homes on one level with a basement and a two-car garage.

In my opinion the world was too green and too quiet out there. No cars or trucks or chatter of voices. No music floated out into the air from bars. And no city smells, street sweat and gas fumes, rubber tires, and burning oil from old beaters that drank more oil than gas. Nope, not for me thank you.

When we got to Al's, we unloaded. Once in the house, Jack went through the hand shaking and hugging bit. I gave him my spare .45 and box of shells. Shelly had her .38.

I made sure the detective was good on what he was supposed to do and told them I had to go.

Shelly grabbed me and kissed me. Jack grinned. He and Al ushered Allie off into the kitchen with her complaining all the way.

"Be careful Max," Shelly urged, and hugged me hard.

"I intend to, Kitten." I hugged her back.

"I know but–" she said, beginning to tear up. I held her real close. The smell and the heat from her made me feel like the luckiest man in the world. I kissed her long and sweet, and then let her go and walked to the door. Outside, Jack was standing on the porch. He had walked around the house to keep from disturbing our goodbye. He smoked a cigar as I stopped beside him.

"Welcome home cigar from Al," Jack said with a puff.

"Do you love her, Max?"

I stopped and looked him in the eye. "Like nobody else can."

"Then watch your ass, buddy. She lost one love a long time ago. That's where the angel came from. It was back when the bosses were overrunning the unions in New York. He was a dock worker. That's why we moved here; to get away and to help her heal."

"And has she?"

"Oh yeah, I do believe she has." He smiled and held out his hand.

I shook it and told him I would kick his ass if anything happened to her. He laughed and continued puffing the cigar as he watched me back out and drive away.

CHAPTER 13

I pulled up to the front of the Station and started to cut the motor when Pat and Trent barreled out the door and saw me.

"What's up?" I called to them as they piled into the car.

Pat jumped into the passenger seat and slammed the door. "Somebody tried to kill our buddy, Gino, again.

I tossed the car in gear and pulled out fast. My tires squealed on the hot pavement as I hauled ass toward City Hospital and hoped the goons missed their mark.

There were police cruisers and cops all over the hospital parking lot when we got there. One nurse gave one of Pat's men hell over the noise they were making. One of his detectives, Kenny, met him when we entered the lobby, the nurse hot on his heels.

"This is a hospital, gentlemen," she growled at Pat and the detective. "Respect and quiet are the rules here!"

"I'll keep that in mind," Pat growled back, "Now if you don't mind…"

He pulled the detective away to talk to him. The nurse

started to follow. I stepped between them. Her eyes locked on mine.

"I ain't as polite as he is." My voice was low, my eyes never left hers. "Now, shove off, sister and let us do our jobs!'

She broke eye contact with me, mumbling something about the D.A. and the chief of staff in the hospital. I pulled a cigar from my pocket and clamped it between my teeth. One of the nurses passed by gave me the thumbs up. I grinned and joined Pat and Kenny who explained what was going on.

"They have him in surgery." Kenny rubbed the back of his neck.

"What happened?" Pat asked.

"This male orderly came by with dinner, took a tray into his room while I was sitting by the door. He was there maybe two, three minutes and came out, leaned against the cart. I heard something clack against the handle of the cart when he leaned in to push it. Never thought nothing about it till another cart came by and the girl took out a tray to take to Gino. That's when it dawned on me that guy was a fake. I went in and he had a knife wound in his chest. The doc said the blade just missed his heart, but there could be other damage, so they took him to surgery. Sorry, Pat," Kenny ducked his head.

Pat didn't reply. We went up to the second floor and talked to the nurse on duty. She couldn't tell us anything more than what Kenny told us. Trent was there also, talking to the other nurses on the floor.

Pat and I found the waiting room and poured some coffee, that turned out to be more like diesel fuel than Joe. I sipped once, then tossed the rest in the trash then took a seat. "Did you tell Trent about Gino being here in the hospital?"

"Yeah, I filled him in on our episode and he was there when they called in that Gino had been stabbed."

"Ok, so he reports back to his office and they report to whoever, right?"

"Yeah, I suppose so. What are you getting at, Max?"

"There is a leak somewhere."

"How do you figure?" Pat poured more diesel fuel from the pot then sat beside me.

"I believe this is a cover up. It started with us finding the girl then this. But I don't think it has anything to do with Holton."

"Your gut again?"

"That, and why would Holton off his guys just because they screwed up? No, there is something more to this. Anything on the prints yet?"

"Not yet. Trent is still trying to get them pushed through."

"Yeah, right." I didn't trust the guy.

"Do you think maybe Trent–?"

I rubbed a hand over my face thinking Holton wouldn't have whacked his men. He would have laid low, let his men take the wrap, and denied knowing anything about it. "I don't know, but I do know someone who might be able to fill me in." I stood, we needed to check this out.

Pat sat back in his chair, swirling the coffee around in the cup. He sipped it again, scowled and then tossed it in the trash like I did. "So you think she's still around?" Pat stood also.

I nodded, pleased he knew who I referred to. "Yeah, I do, but changed. I'd say that picture I have is ten years old maybe older. A girl can look way different in ten years, especially if she wants to disappear. Change hair color, slim down...hell, she might even have a little surgery to change her face some. She is the key here, old buddy. I just can't figure out how or why."

"Ok, so there aren't that many plastic surgeons here in town. Should be easy to check."

Now he was thinking. "Well, not many with a license

to do the job," I said, "That's where I come in."

I walked to the door, opened it then stepped out. I needed to see a friend of mine. He'd know who practiced the face changing profession without a diploma. I turned toward Pat. "I'll check some things out. Want a ride back to the department."

"No, you go on. I'll hitch a ride with one of the patrolmen when I'm ready."

In the parking lot, I crawled into my heap and started it up. I kept trying to figure where the leak was. Trent's name drifted in and out of my mind while I drove. Something deep inside me didn't trust him. I didn't have a clue why, but would keep that filed away for now and hope it wasn't true.

***

I went back to the office and upstairs to the room I had once occupied before I met Shelly. I cleaned up, changed my shirt and laid down for a bit before going to see my friend.

All of a sudden the fatigue hit me. I glanced around the old room. It reminded me just how good things had gotten since I met Shelly. Now, the room was nothing but a dust collector. Shelly came up once a week and checked things out, just in case we needed to use it again. I chuckled as I thought of me thinking, "we".

I was a confirmed bachelor before her, and wonder if and when we tie the knot, whether things will drastically change. I mean, even now if I come in smelling like perfume or have a smudge of lipstick on my collar, not that I've done anything because I haven't, but sometimes dames think they can make points by trying to kiss me, I get the cold shoulder for a couple of weeks. No matter how I explain it, she just grunts and continues to work. I finally decided to not to make try to convince her I'm innocent. I just make sure I'm showered and change to a clean shirt before I make my entrance.

Outside, the sounds of voices and a cars passing came through the open window. The sounds of the city caused me to drift off to sleep. Hours later I woke up in a sweat, the room hot as a pistol. It was dark, and when I looked at my watch it told me it was after midnight. I sat up on the edge of the bed, ran my hands through my hair, stood and went to the sink. I twisted the handle and let the water run for a few minutes, hoping it would get cooler. It didn't, so I washed off the sweat and put on another clean shirt.

That little thought came back again, gnawing around the edges of my consciousness. I walked downstairs to the cabinet where I kept my ammo, took out a box of shells and a couple more clips, and loaded them. Still couldn't remember. I slipped into another jacket and slid the clips in the pocket. This trace had turned into a nightmare for me, and anyone associated with me. I leaned back in my chair and thought back to all that had happened, trying to put some order to it. There was none.

These last boys were heavy hitters, and if Holton was trying to sweep something else under the rug besides a simple trace, I was sure as hell going to find out what it was.

I left the office, the heat outside a little better than inside. As I locked the door, a couple of winos staggered past me. The smell of cheap booze and twenty years of dirt touched my nostrils. Funny how these guys always appear at night, like vampires, but their life-giving sustenance was sucked from a bottle. Once that was gone they went to either bugging, begging or finding someone who would share their lust for the life- giving fluid.

A young couple was coming toward them. One of the drinkers pulled himself upright, stepped in front of the couple and demanded a dollar. The girl did the perfect movie pose. She stopped and gasped. Her hand covered her mouth as her eyes widened. The guy took a step forward. The wino's buddy slipped past him and around behind. These guys were either desperate or just plain stupid. I stopped and pulled out a cigar, scratched a match on my thumbnail and lit up. The backdoor wino saw me, turned and walked away first slow and then faster as he got farther away.

"Happy, you damned coward" the one I was standing behind yelled.

"No, he was smart," I said. He jerked around, staggered and almost fell.

"Beat it buddy, or..."

I grinned and then he recognized me. His mouth dropped open and his eyes bugged.

"Hey Max." The smell of his breath enough to make a sober man drunk. "I was just foolin' around you know and..."

"You got five seconds before I call a cop," I blew smoke in his face. He turned, doffed his hat to the lady and took off. I laughed and told the two kids to get where they were going before the booze made the two drunks brave again. They thanked me and I hustled on toward Kelso's.

CHAPTER 14

I walked the three doors down to Kelso's and stepped into his establishment. The heat was churned, the same as it was in a lot of establishments, by the slow moving ceiling fans. Kelso's was one of the bars that catered to a rougher crowd. His bar was at the back, a big walnut job that had scars from the years past decorating its surface; one of them, a bullet hole, my bullet hole, the lead still in the bar. There was a crack in mirror behind the bar that looked like a glass spider web. The story behind that we will save for another time.

Kelso's was the favorite haunt of the soiled doves who worked this side of town, coming out only when the sun set, which was a good thing, if you catch my drift. A few of them were already there, trying to get me to buy them a drink, which would lead to more enjoyable things for some. Not me. I'd have to be awful drunk to go home with one of them, awful drunk. Fisk sat at his usual booth, last one on the right side.

Fisk was the man to see when I wanted to know what was happening in the city. Standing at about 5'4", a muscular, but small man, his arms thick and corded and his hands, when made into fists, looked like small sledge hammers. From what I heard, felt like them, too. I slid into his booth and he glanced up. His eyes narrowed. Dark eyes that told a fellow he was not one to fool around with.

Fisk and I have been friends for a long time. My first case he had helped me get the goods on, was when a no good hood who tried to frame me for killing a girl I knew and Fisk liked. Fisk led me to the man and I took care of business. The funeral home mortician suggested a closed casket since there wasn't much of a face left to morn over.

"Word is you have stepped on some big toes, my friend," Fisk said in a low voice.

"I figured as much. Who?" I asked.

"Locals and out-of-towners."

"Holton?"

"Nope."

"Is that so," I sat back and looked at him long and hard. "And the dead girl?"

Fisk shrugged "Nothing. At least nothing on the vine. Listen Max, these boys are big league. Holton is small stuff. If it was me, I'd let the Gates' girl go before you or someone associated with you gets waxed."

"Too late for that. They crossed my line, and you know how I am when that happens. Besides, I won't believe the dead girl is Gates' till we get the prints back."

"Your gut?"

"Yeah."

He grinned. "Look, these boys are from New York and not part of Holton's crew. They have been here for a long time; I'm surprised they've kept such a low profile for this long. They have local connections here, boys that have been on their payroll since Prohibition days."

"Any idea who?'

"The main one is in a high city office. His second in command, is connected with the law."

"Connected or is?"

"That I haven't been able to find out. Every time I get close, the information source dries up."

The waitress came by. "What can I get you , honey."

I glanced up at her. "Nothing, thanks."

"Suit yourself." She walked away, I'm sure sorry she missed a tip.

Fisk stirred his cocktail. "Anything else?"

"Yeah, any face jobs been done in the past few years by an unlicensed sawbones?"

"None that I know of but I can ask around."

I stood and stuck my hand in my pocket, palmed a fin and passed it off when we shook.

"Watch your back, Max. Don't cross the line."

I nodded and left.

CHAPTER 15

Line? I have a line. They crossed it when they tried to hurt Shelly and my other friends. The night was still hot, the pavement even hotter under my feet. I leaned against a light post and lit another cigar. If the big boys he was talking about had of been Samson Baxter's crew, Fisk would of said, hell, Samson would of already cornered me, not try and kill me. Like he said, Holton is small time.

I bounced off the lamp post and started toward the office when the sound of a car picking up speed came to my ears. High beams blinded me for a second. It was a green Ford. A man in the back pointed a trench gun out the window.

I dove to the sidewalk just as the trench gun shattered the still air. The car came to a screeching halt. I had my .45 out with hammer cocked. One of the men from the car stepped from around the vehicle I was behind. I put two into him at close range. He fell on his ass as red rain spattered the air behind him.

I flipped over on my back and saw another snub nosed .38 over the hood of the same car. He went down with one in his head. It was then I heard a shell pumped into a second trench gun. I rolled over and tried to melt into the car body, hoping he'd hit more of the sidewalk than of me but doubting it. I was about to take a chance and do another roll across the side walk toward the buildings, but he never got to pull the trigger. Fisk pumped both barrels of a sawed off double trench into him, knocked his ass halfway down the sidewalk. Fisk nodded to me and came to help me stand up.

"Told you to watch your back!" he said in a low voice.

"Yeah, thanks."

He smiled. "You're welcome." He walked back to Kelso's, the shotgun on his shoulder, and damned if he wasn't whistling!

CHAPTER 16

"**H**ell, Max, it would have been nice if you'd have left one of them alive to question," Pat said as they bagged the bodies.

"I'll keep that in mind for next time."

"And the last guy, double ought buckshot. Where did that come from?"

"Maybe one of them missed me and hit his partner." I couldn't rat on Fisk. The man saved my life.

"Uh-huh."

Trent looked over the dead and made notes. He shook his head and came over to where we stood.

"You always leave a trail of dead when you work a case?" He was looking straight at me.

"Oh, he most certainly does," a voice said behind us before I could answer.

I turned and Detective Matt Perkins was there. He wore a nasty smile. Perkins walked past us and turned to face me, the smile faded. Perkins is an ugly little man, no scars or anything, just plain butt ugly. He was about a hundred pounds overweight for his short frame.

The man has a moon shaped face, flabby cheeks and a pointed nose that would pop a balloon if he got too close. His suits were top of the line, tailored to fit his flabby frame. How he afforded them on a detective's salary.... He couldn't, so he had to be dirty. We all knew he was, but couldn't prove it. He stepped in close and a big grin crossed his lips when he spoke to me.

"One of these days, Black, you're gonna screw up and I am gonna be all over you," he hissed.

Trent gave me a puzzled look as my eyes narrowed. "What the hell are you talking about, Perkins?" I stared into his eyes and saw hate in them, a bad hate.

"Look around you." The fat man waved his arms. "A gunfight in the middle of a business district in the middle of the night? Some drunk might have staggered out of one of the bars and gotten killed besides these fellows. Yeah, you're gonna screw up and you're gonna fall, and your buddy, Mr. Peterson, is not gonna be able to help you."

"Next time I'll call a time out and we'll move to a more suitable location," I growled back at him and matched his stare.

"I oughta…"

"You oughta what?" Pat came up behind him. Matt turned toward him and smirked, then walked off.

I looked at Pat, then at Perkins. I made a fist and started toward him. Pat grabbed me and held me back. I stopped took in a deep breath and let it out slowly.

Matt Perkins held me and Al responsible for his not getting the Captain's job. See, Abe Howard, the Chief of Police, and D.A. Bledsoe were going to give it to him until Al and I convinced them, along with a few others, he was not the man for the job. Like I said, Perkins was dirty. Howard and everybody knew it but no one would flip on him. If someone was willing, they couldn't be found.

It came to me through the grapevine that Perkins claimed one night while talking to some of his buddies during a card game that he would someday have me in a chair in the interrogation room and when he got done with me, even that little whore I was sleeping with wouldn't recognize me. I made it clear to said buddies to tell him that before that happened I would make him a worst mess than me before he hauled me in.

"I take it he doesn't have fond feelings for you, Mr. Black?" Trent stepped up beside me as Perkins walked away.

"You think?" I unclenched my fist and walked away. Trent was getting on my nerves.

I rode with Pat back to the Station to give a statement, and dropped in the chair beside his desk. He fumbled with some papers then sat back and ran his fingers through his hair.

"I have a mind to put Perkins on foot patrol for the comments he made," Pat leaned back in his chair.

"Yeah, but that would only make it worse," I shifted so my rig didn't bite into my side when I leaned on his desk. "Besides, you know he's dirty. Just how dirty? Well..."

"You think he—"

"How's Shelly doing?" I changed the subject and I wanted to know. I missed her.

"Worried sick about you." Pat took a deep breath then let it out. "Allie says she at least once every hour says she misses you terribly. It's nice to have a woman like that, huh?"

"Yeah, it is, and I miss her, too."

There was a knock at Pat's door and Kenny came in. He handed Pat a file folder.

"Trent sent this over. You're not gonna believe this." He waited till Pat opened the folder.

Pat let out a low whistle and shook his head. "Two of those' boys you and Jack took out that night at Shelly's were from the New York Mob." He kept reading. "Tony and Jimmy Russo." He looked at me. "The third was Ben

Valerio, one of Samson's men."

I sat up in my chair and took the sheet from Pat. Ben Valerio was one of Samson's enforcers, although Samson denied it. He claimed Valerio was the vice-president of Samson's Imports.

"I think I need to see a man about an employee," I tossed the paper back on Pat's desk.

Pat had a serious look on his face. "Want some company?"

"No, Samson might not be as social if you are with me," I saw Pat nod, then I exited the office. Perkins watched me as I walked by his desk, a shit eating grin plastered on his face. He turned toward me, leaned back in his chair and folded his arms across his fat belly.

"Something on your mind, wiseass?" His smirk widening.

"Yeah," Real quick I dipped my hand under my coat. Perkins tensed then relaxed when I pulled out a cigar. "You owe me an apology."

"For what?" His eyes narrow.

I struck a match and lit the stogie. "Well, not to me to Shelly, for calling her a whore," A wicked smile crossed my face.

"The hell—"

I flipped the match at him. Perkins batted at it when the smoldering stick landed on his vest, which led to his fat ass over-balancing in the office chair, and caused him to fall backwards. It sounded like a clap of thunder as he landed on his back on the floor.

"That'll do." I stalked out and couldn't stop laughing.

CHAPTER 17

Samson's Imports is in the old Timpson's Furniture Factory, a big two story brick building on the corner of Jefferson and Traffic Way. It had gone bust during the crash an stood empty until Samson bought it and opened up his "business." Samson claimed to be in the business of importing rare and valuable antiques from all over the world. There were a few pieces scattered around the warehouse, along with a couple of delivery trucks and a few men that seemed to be standing around more in the dock doors trying to cool off than working. I guess since the war, business was a little lax.

I walked up to the door and buzzed the buzzer. After several minutes, I pushed it and held it till one of his goons, Lenny, jerked the door open. Lenny and I have had a few rounds together in years past. He is Samson's muscle.

"What the hell do you want, shamus?" he barked.

"Well, hello to you too, Lenny. I need to talk to Samson."

"What if he don't want to talk to you?"

Tell him it has something to do with one of his boys.

Coleman, to be specific."

Lenny motioned me in, then closed the door. "You carryin'?"

"Does a bear piss in the woods?" He knew damn good an well I had a gun on me.

"Hand it over,"

I pulled out my .45 and handed it to him, butt first. He looked it over then stuffed it in his belt.

"You should have checked the safety before you shoved that cannon in your pants?"

"Why?"

"Hate to be the cause of you not being able to sire any kids. Although that might be a good thing."

He slowly pulled the gun out and looked at it. The safety was on. I laughed and he mumbled something under his breath then shoved the firearm back into his waistband.

One side of the warehouse had been sectioned off. The company name was painted above the only door, in old English letters. I grabbed the door knob and pulled. It was like going from slums into where royalty resided.

The reception room was done in light mahogany planks waist high around the walls, tongue and grooved together and polished to a soft sheen. Above that the walls had been painted a pale gray. A table sat along the left wall, one that cost probably more money than I could make in my lifetime. It looked European, the curves and swirls gave it that old world look. Chairs lined the right wall, comfortable leather and dark wood jobs, the kind you see in old men's clubs, the kind that when you set in them for a while you drifted off to sleep.

Behind a mile wide desk sat his secretary. She looked up and smiled. She was a busty blonde, a little heavy on the makeup, but a doll just the same.

She pushed a button on the intercom and spoke. "You have a visitor, Mr. Samson."

That was where I had to bite my lip. Her squeaky voice

grated on my nerves. How could a man wake up to that sound every morning?

"Send him in."

She stood, walked to the door, opened it then nodded for me to enter. I did as instructed.

I stepped inside and let out a low whistle. The same wall coverings were in the office, mahogany and pale gray, but the rest was like out of a picture book from Hollywood. Oriental rugs covered the floor. An antique side board set to my right. To my left was a beautiful teak wood table. The same kind of chairs sat in front of his desk, and another cabinet sat to the left of his desk. Two or three pictures hung on the walls, all of them of a boxer pounding the hell out of someone. Samson came around his desk and stuck out a big hand. I took it and shook with him.

I had only seen Samson once, and that was from a distance, and then he looked big. Samson weighted maybe 290, stood about 5'8" inches tall and was a broad chested brute. His arms were muscular and you could see the muscles beneath his shirt, twist and untwist like coils of rope as he shook my hand.

His grip was a vice. He had a boxer's face, nose flat, his gray eyes staring from permanently puffed brows and one of his ears was the shape of a cauliflower. I supposed the pictures on the wall were of him. He smiled and a gold tooth sparkled where one had been knocked out. The only reason I was talking to him was because he owed me big time as I kept a bullet from ending his career one night.

"Welcome, Mr. Black. What can I do for you?" He pumped my arm twice and then turned loose. I was glad he did. A couple a more pumps and I do believe I would have spouted water.

"Coleman," I said simply.

He nodded and walked back around his desk and sat down. "Very unfortunate," He offered me a cigar from his humidor.

I took it, a black job that smelled musky and stout. I stuck it in my shirt pocket. "Thanks."

"Benny wasn't happy here with us." Samson paused to light his cigar. Blue gray smoke rose above his head. "He resigned."

"Yeah, right into a New York gig."

Samson shrugged. "I see. Well, what he did after he left here was his own decision." He took another long pull on the cigar. "But I am sorry he met with a bad fate. Especially when it comes to you. Lenny has told me a bit about you, Mr. Black."

He leaned forward and grinned. "I must say that at least you haven't shot any of my men, Coleman excluded." He laughed. "Let me be frank. Benny was on the run because certain finances were coming up short. He skimmed me. I don't have to tell you that's a no-no. I pay my people well, and for one of them to steal from me is an unforgivable insult."

"A deadly insult," I added.

Samson chuckled. "Yes, possibly so. Why he was with those men is beyond me, although there must have been a reason for it." He blew more smoke.

I eyed Samson for a moment. My gut told me he was lying. Something else was in the works here because if Coleman had been stealing from Samson he would have already been dead.

"And that reason would be?" I pressed.

Sampson sat back in his chair. "Maybe whoever he was working for made him a better offer."

"Uh-huh."

"Listen Max, you opened a can of worms when you went to look for this girl. And don't look surprised, word gets around," he said his face serious. "Certain people might not want this person found because it will involve the fall of certain people who are very upright in this city, and would make a spectacle of it, especially with the business they are in. There are people in high places that would do anything to keep this out of the public eye, to keep this business going. A very nasty business, Max, one I would never get involved in and yes, I know what they are involved in, but let's just keep that between us, shall we?"

"So the dead girl isn't Gates?" I asked.

"That is for you to find out." He cut his eyes sideways toward me.

"Even a hint?" I asked.

He shook his head no and leaned on his desk. His eyes narrowed. "And this squares it between us."

I nodded and stood as he pressed the intercom button.

"Trixie, come see Mr. Black out, please."

"Yes, Mr. Baxter," she squeaked. Samson flinched.

"Least she has the body," I said with a smirk.

"Yes, at least." Samson shook his head "She wants to be a singer."

I walked toward the door. "And you're helping her?"

"Like you said, at least she has the body."

Trixie came in and ushered me out the door.

CHAPTER 18

I sat in my office and thought about what Sampson had said. It was a nasty business, something that would pull certain people down and make this city a spectacle once it was discovered; people who knew where I was and where the hoods could find me. People who didn't want me to find Becky Gates because she might lead me to whatever this nasty business was and who was behind it.

I racked my brain. Wondered what these people were into and who they were. Drugs were a nasty business. I had seen many a good man hooked and turned into a shell of what he used to be, the long stares and the shakes, mugging people for money. The urge to get a fix driving a man to kill, and sometimes it was someone close to them who denied them the money for their nirvana.

But I had a feeling this was bigger than drugs. Samson dealt in nothing stronger than Marijuana, happy weed some call it, and if he caught any of his boys dealing in anything stronger, they ended up with broken fingers. No, my gut told me it was something bigger and as Sampson had said, nastier.

When it came to nasty, only one someone came to mind. But without proof, that someone was sitting in the clear and laughing his ass off at me. I leaned back in my chair, laced my fingers behind my head and let that thought run around in my head for a fast second or two, then stopped it before it drove me crazy.

The office was still hot, but not as hot as during the day. I switched off the fan perched on the corner of my desk as blew nothing but hot air on me and sat up. This case was about to get the best of me. I had had only one or two that had done this to me before. One was a wife killer, and the other was a dope peddler. I stayed with them, though, and finally came out on top.

But this one, this one had more variables, more people threatened than back then. I walked to the front and switched off the lights, then went back to switch off the light on my desk, when pounding about to shatter the glass in the door spun me around.

Pat yelled for me to let him in. I quickly opened the door and he grabbed me.

"They hit Al's house," he said jerking me toward the door, "Al was shot, so was Jack and–"

"Shelly?" My heart sank.

"Shot, but not bad, she took out two of them before they took off. They left a warning note tacked to the doorpost telling you to back off before someone you loved ended up in the grave!"

***

Shelly had taken one in the arm, through and through, and Al had gotten peppered by some buckshot. Jack was the one who had taken the worst, two in the side and one in the leg. He was in surgery. Shelly was asleep. Allie and Al sat with her. I stepped in and they nodded. I leaned over and kissed Shelly lightly on the lips.

"Oh, Max." Al pulled me out into the hall.

"What happened?"

Al's arm was bandaged from the elbow to his wrist. "They pulled up in a cruiser and the detective on watch went out to see what they wanted. I heard shots and ran to the window. The detective was down. Four of them came toward the house; one still sat in the car. Jack and Shelly were coming out of the kitchen when they burst through the door. Jack took out the first one, right through the heart. The second put two in his side, but Shelly shot him between the eyes. You taught her well, Max.

"The third came in low and fired a shotgun. Missed me and Shelly cause I shoved her out of the way as I dove for the floor. I got my arm peppered but he took two from me in the chest. That was when I saw him, crouched by the door. He poked his gun in and fired off three rounds. One of them hit Shelly in the arm, the other hit Jack in the leg. I fired toward him but he was up and running toward the car. I guess the detective was still alive because he grabbed him by the leg. The guy spun and shot the detective in the head! It was Perkins, Max!"

"Does Pat know this?"

"Yeah, I told him. He said he'd put out an all points on him."

Trent came down the hall talking to one of the doctors. The doc nodded and took off down the other hall. Trent walked up to us. "The kid was lucky. The two slugs in his side missed anything vital and the one in his leg went straight through. I told the doc to see he got the best of care."

"Thanks," Al said, shaking his hand. "How's your lady?" he asked me.

"Sleeping." I turned, went back into Shelly's room and sat down on the edge of her bed. Allie left me to watch her sleep. Told me she was going with Al to wait for when Jack go out of surgery. I brushed a lock of stray hair off my girl's forehead and then kissed her again. A smile crossed her face. I stood and sat down in the chair next to the bed. The day had been a long one; the quiet of the room closed in on me and put me to sleep.

***

"Well, well," I heard a voice say. I jerked awake and my hand went for the grip of my .45, but it wasn't there. "How you doing, sleeping beauty? You must have been really tired for me to relieve you of this."

Matt Perkins sat on the edge of Shelly's bed, my .45 in his hand, tapping the muzzle against Shelly's leg. I sat up and eyed him. My fist clenched, ready to see if I could knock his ass off the bed before he shot one of us. He pointed the .45 at her head.

"Go ahead, wiseass, try it. One twitch and your whore is dead!"

I relaxed and he lowered the gun.

"You are a hard man to kill, Max, a hard man to kill."

"How did you get in?"

"Lots of ways in a hospital besides the front door, Max."

"And the cop on watch?"

"He was relieved."

"I bet."

"Well, what can I say?" A big grin spread across his face.

"So what comes next?"

"Well." He pulled a silencer from his jacket pocket, screwed it onto my .45. "Oh, and thanks for having a threaded barrel on this piece; thought I might have to use a pillow. 'Course they aren't as quiet."

"So what's your plan, fat boy?" I hoped to make him mad so he'd do something stupid. His face went red but he never moved, just gripped the gun harder and snarled at me.

"I've been thinking about that. See, what's gonna happen is I'm gonna pop you in the chest, then shoot your whore between the eyes just before you die, and waltz out of here as cool as the breeze."

He leveled the gun at me. Behind him I saw Shelly's hand inch over to one of those metal barf pans lying beside her.

"Pat will find you," I said, stalling for time. I wanted his eyes on me as she moved to grip the pan.

"Well, he'll have to live long enough to do it, and my other boss will make sure that won't happen. See, you and that piss-ant Irishman shouldn't of cheated me out of the Captain's job. I had plans, we both did, and they all went down the drain when that Mick took over." he growled in a low voice.

Shelly gripped the pan, her eyes slits.

"Big plans?" I leaned slightly forward in the chair and braced my feet against the floor. I needed to keep him talking. In this state, he might just slip.

"Oh yes, that little escapade with Al at the rail station, when he was still Chief of Detectives, wasn't just a happenstance. It was planned to get him out of the way and, possibly you in the same instance. Too bad it didn't work."

So Perkins was in on that ordeal. He referred to the very case that led to Al's retirement. Both of us damned near bought it during that one.

"Since then we have been watching your every move, Max. There are others besides me watching you, too. We set our trap for you and you slipped out of it by the skin of your teeth! Hell, I even tried to get there before Pat did. If I had of, I would have taken you out along with that snitch you have at Kelso's. But shit happens, so I tried to get you to assault me, and even that didn't work. I wanted to make good my threat, remember?"

"Yeah, I remember."

He shook, his rage and hate for me were burning him

up. "So what kept you from making it before Pat?"

He started to speak and then stopped. A smile crossed his lips and his eyes looked wild. "Let's just say I was detained. So long, Max." His smile widened into a lunatic grin. He cocked the hammer.

I had one chance and if Shelly didn't get it right I was gonna take a bullet. He leveled the .45 and Shelly swung the pan. It came down on his wrist. The fingers of his hand opened and the .45 spit out a slug as it dropped to the bed. The slug dug a hole in the wall. He cussed, backhanded her and reached for the gun with his other hand.

I was out of the chair and on him before he could grab it. My right fist caught him on the chin and snapped his head back. My left fist slammed into his jaw and knocked him off the bed. He hit the floor, rolled and came up fast, a snub nose in his hand from a belt holster under his coat but I was quicker. He paused when he saw the .45 in my hand pointed at his head.

"Bang," I said softly. The back of his head showered the room when the bullet went in small and came out big. I knew he wasn't going to move. Ever.

I kept the .45 palmed, but dropped it to my side and held Shelly close for a few moments, Then I pried her loose. "It'll be okay. "

"Close your eyes and don't look at the mess. It's not pretty." I stepped away. "I need to check the hallway." I cracked the door and looked out.

An officer stood at the nurse's desk. His uniform was right but his shoes were all wrong. The nurse tried to head toward Shelly's room, saying she had heard something. The fake cop told her he would do it, and started to walk toward the door.

I told Shelly to scream. She did. The nurse jerked her head toward the door. She bolted from the desk toward the door and I leaped out. The cop, saw it was me instead of Perkins and pulled his piece.

I put one in his shoulder and another in his leg; that folded him. Trent had been talking to the doc when I came out of the room. He saw the cop go down, try and lift his piece to fire. Trent was behind him in a flash, a sap in his hand, tapping the fake cop on the head. A meaty thump sounded loud in the hallway. The fake cop grunted and went out.

"What the hell!" Trent exclaimed, and flipped the cop on his back. Pat and a detective came running, then slid to a stop and looked at the cop.

"One of yours?" Trent asked.

"Nope," Pat looked at me and then back at the cop. "How..."

"His shoes," I said, pointing. "Since when did wingtips become standard issue? "

"So how come he isn't dead?" Trent asked.

"I guess I was feeling generous. Left you a live one for questioning."

I motioned Pat over to the side. "Perkins tried to snuff me and Shelly out."

Pat frowned. "When? How?"

A few minutes ago. That's what started all of this. He's in Shelly's room, unfortunately, his brains are scattered all over the wall.

My friend swore under his breath. "Shit. You shot him in the head?"

What did he expect? "just like he had intended to do to me and Shelly." I heard the door to Shelly's room open.

She came out in her hospital gown, still groggy from pain killers, but stumbled to me and wrapped her arms around me. I picked her up and held her tight.

The nurse started into the room, I tried to warn her not to go inside. Too late.

She came out green around the gills and ran toward the head she didn't make it. She spewed right there on the floor. Must have been a newbie because most nurses have seen a lot of shit and have steel guts, or so I've been told.

After we had Shelly settled in another room and the doctors checked her out, I slipped Al Matt's .38, and asked the doc where the hood I'd shot in the hall was. The doc told me the man was getting patched up and that Pat and Agent Trent were with him. I nodded and told him to take me there.

CHAPTER 19

Pat and Trent stood outside the hood's door, talking, when we came up. Trent talked to the doc and he nodded back and walked away. Pat and I had a puzzled look on our faces as we watched the doc check for nurses along the hall. And those he did find, he spoke to for a second then they hurried off. Once the hall was clear, Trent grinned.

"Let's go have a talk with Mr. Tony Deland," he said, pushing the door open.

Deland was cuffed to the bed, both sides. His shoulder and leg had been bandaged and he was breathing heavy. A spot of blood showed through both bandages. Trent had convinced them to let the slugs stay for a while. Just slow the bleeding.

He was the typical goon. His jaw tightened when we came in. He wasn't a bad looking fellow, one of those rugged looking guys with eyes that drilled into us.

Trent walked up to his bed. "Hello, Tony,"

The man's eyes narrowed and he clenched his fists. My gut told me he knew Trent. I was right.

"Tony and I have a little history," Trent continued. "I

sent him up five years... for possession... back when he was younger. Ain't that right, Tony?"

Tony grunted.

"Now." Trent moved closer. He reached in his pocket and pulled out the sap, a piece of leather with a lead weight sewn in the end of it for those who need to know. The end drooped from the extra weight in it. "I'm gonna ask you a few questions, that ok?"

"Kiss my ass!" Tony looked at the sap, then at Trent. "You can't do that to me, and there are witnesses...."

He suddenly realized that what he was going to say was of no use. Trent raised the sap and let it fall lightly on Tony's good leg. The sap landed and Tony flinched.

"Not a good attitude to have Tony," Trent said, his voice hard.

Pat looked at me, then Trent. I grinned and crossed my arms over my chest. I might not trust him, but he was good.

"What's the dope, Tony, why all the hits? Looks like someone is trying to eliminate people for some reason. Max here must be close to something. What is it?"

Tony just stared. Trent gave the sap a flick and it snapped up and then down, the meaty thud of it hit his good thigh, the sound loud in the room. Tony's eyes bugged, he gritted his teeth and a hiss of air came out from between his lips.

"Tony's a tough one, boys," Trent said, "but not tough enough. Next one lands on the shoulder."

He moved the sap over to the wounded shoulder and let it hover over the wound. Tony's eyes widened and his face went pale.

"Last chance." Trent raised the sap.

Tony's mouth worked, the words coming out dry as dust.

"I was told to meet Perkins outside the hospital for a job." He licked his lips and watched the sap. "Perkins had the uniform and told me to change into it. Then we came up here."

"The cop on watch?" I asked.

"Yeah, Perkins had me dump him in the incinerator," Tony said.

Pat stepped out in the hall and told the cop by the door to get some help and go look.

"Did you know Perkins was gonna shoot Max and the girl?" Trent asked.

"He only told me he had some unfinished business to tend to. He said he was gonna take care of a pain in his ass," he said in a whimper, the sap closer to the wound.

"Who does he work for?" Pat asked, his voice tense.

Tony shook his head. "I don't know that's the honest truth!"

Trent let the sap touch the wound and Tony's mouth opened but nothing came out.

"Better not be lying," Trent moved even closer.

"Look, Trent." The man's eyes were glued to the sap. "There are only a handful that know who the kingpins are. The hired help only get their orders from the guys under the kingpins."

Trent nodded and raised the sap a bit, then took it and placed it back in his pocket. "Ok Tony. You just relax and get better, okay?"

Tony cursed and lunged at Trent. The cuffs stopped him but the motion caused the blood spots on his leg and arm to grow brighter. Trent laughed and we exited the room.

"Reminds me of me," I said in a low voice to Pat as we went out.

"Yeah, that's all I need right now is another you." He shook his head.

CHAPTER 20

"He'll be out by tomorrow," Trent speculated. He sat on the couch in Pat's office. "Wounded or not, they will spring him. Whoever they are, they probably have connections."

"He has an attempted murder charge along with impersonating a cop charge against him," Pat said. "And the bail was set extremely high."

"Like I said, he will be out tomorrow."

"So what do we do?" I queried.

"When he makes bail, and he will make bail, we'll follow him and see where he goes after he is cut loose. He might just lead us to one of the bosses."

"Yeah, he really didn't give us a damned thing to go on." Pat leaned back in his chair and steepled his fingers.

The air was pretty stiff in Pat's office; the humidity had thickened in the night and the fan just cut and tossed chunks out in wet, heated air.

"Unless it was Perkins himself. You heard what he said, only a handful know who the real bosses are behind this. Maybe Perkins was one of them." Trent said.

"Yeah," I almost relayed to the two of them what

Sampson had told me, but bit my tongue, I would tell Pat later when we were alone.

"Maybe Perkins was the main guy, I mean, I have suspected him of being dirty so maybe he was the one." Pat said.

"Yeah, I was thinking the same thing," Trent stood. "But I suspect he was just an underling. Look, I need to check in so I'll see you guys tomorrow."

I nodded as he exited the office. There was something that still bothered me about Trent. What I couldn't put my finger on. But I would, you could bet your damned last dollar I would!

CHAPTER 21

The next day storm clouds built in the northwest, big black ones. Heat lighting arched across their bellies like red, wicked tongues.

I filled Pat in on what Sampson had told me, then Pat got the call that Edward Boone was there to make bail for Tony. Tony had already been released from the hospital and now sat in a cell.

Pat went downstairs and checked out the paper work Boone had brought to make it all legal. He then told them to cut him loose. Trent was there and he and I went down the street to where Trent's car was parked a couple of spots down from the entrance of the Station. The plan was to follow him and see where he went.

Tony and Boone came out a few minutes later. Tony walked with a cane, his arm in a sling. They talked for a few moments and then Tony hopped in the cab Boone had come in and slammed the door before Boone could get in. Boone yelled that he was a despicable fellow. Tony laughed as the cab pulled away. Boone stomped back in the Station and we followed the cab.

The driver took a roundabout route through the city. Trent kept at least two cars back from the cab at all times. Finally the driver turned onto Jefferson, turned left in front of the Legion Hall and let Tony out in front of Cully's Diner. Trent and I parked at the curb in front of the Colonial. The doorman waltzed out to the car and looked in. Trent held his buzzer up and told the doorman to take a hike.

Tony went in, talked with the waitress for a minute, and then sat down at the counter. Bert came out after that. He was dressed different, a shirt covered his chest instead of the usual undershirt. He looked a little heavier in the chest, thicker. He leaned on the counter and started talking. Suddenly Bert straightened up, his face screwed up and his hands gripped the dish towel. Tony stood up and stepped back as Bert pointed a finger and said something, then walked over to the register and opened it. Tony hustled to him. Bert took some money out of the drawer and handed it to him, growled at him again and pointed.

Tony nodded, stuffed the money in his pocket, then left the restaurant. He took out a pack of cigarettes, shook one loose, lit it and looked around for a cab.

A '39 Chevy came roaring down the street as he stood there, the cigarette halfway to his mouth. The blast of a trench gun filled the still air.

It looked like Tony had jumped up to dodge the blast, then a second blast took him in midair and knocked him three feet back. His body bounced on the sidewalk then lay still. Bert ran out, a pistol in his hand but he never got to use it. The blast aimed at him knocked him back into the glass door. People in the restaurant dove for the floor.

At the first shot, Trent started the car and jammed it in gear, popped the clutch and floored it. His old buggy jumped into the path of the Chevy just as it came into the intersection; metal ground and glass shattered.

I opened the door and rolled out, my .45 out of my rig

in the cocked position. Trent followed just as a shotgun blast took out his windshield on the driver's side. Three of them came boiling out of the car, firing at the old heap in front of them as they backed away. I waited for a lull and then popped up. The guy with the trench gun saw me, but too late. I took him out. He staggered backwards as the .45 slugs pounded into him.

Trent traded fire with the other two. One of them had seen the trench gun man go down. He tossed two over the back of the car and then peeked over the trunk. He saw me grin just before he died. The other one ran. Trent popped shots at him; one hit home, the other two knocked chips from the retaining wall he ducked behind.

Trent leaned against the car, tipped back his hat, shook his head as I walked up.

"I had heard talk that things were wicked when you were around and deep in a case. I always thought it was just talk," he said, rubbing his side, "Now I know better."

I grinned and leaned against the car with him. A small crowd gathered, rubber necking the scene as a patrol car screeched to a halt beside us.

CHAPTER 22

The cops set up barricades and pushed people back. Especially the reporters who, like vultures, yelled questions trying to find out what had happened. I walked to where Bert lay on his back through the busted door. I knelt beside him and noticed there was no blood oozing out around him. Then he groaned.

I called to Trent and he hustled over. His eyes narrowed as I pulled back the tattered shirt. Trent knelt down with me and then called for a patrolman who was standing close. He spoke to the man for a few minutes and the cop nodded, walked to where one of the cruisers was parked and pulled it up in front of the diner.

Bert groaned and Trent kneeled down beside him, whispering in his ear. Bert suddenly grew still. We picked him up and loaded him in the car, then drove off down the street. Bert lay in the back, groaning and moaning.

"Wonder where the hell he got the vest?" Trent turned a corner.

I shook my head and looked in the back seat. Bert was sitting up, so I pulled out my .45. His eyes got big and round as I grinned at him and cocked the hammer.

"Where…" Bert started to say.

"Someplace nice and safe," I said as he eyed the .45, "where we can talk."

***

Bert was placed in a cell under guard by two jailers I knew and trusted, and then the two of us went up to Pat's office. Pat was still at the crime scene and probably giving us hell for abandoning him. Trent made a couple of phone calls and then said he had to go. As I watched him exit, I thought about the prints and made my way down to see Sergeant Masters.

Masters was a long timer, his knees and feet bad from the many years he walked a beat. He now had a desk job. He mumbled over some paperwork when I came up on him. His eyes jerked up to me and then back to the paperwork.

"What's on your mind, Max," The Sergeant still fumbled with the papers.

"The fingerprints," I parked on the edge of his desk. "The dead girl's. The Feds ever send anything back on them?"

"How the hell would I know," Masters looked up at me, "That Trent came down and got them, said he would take care of it. Why don't you ask him?"

"Between you and me, I don't trust him."

Masters gave me a slight smile. "Neither do I." His eyes sparked. "So I had Doc do a second set. Sent them to a buddy of mine up Kansas City way. He hasn't got back to me yet, so when he does I let you know."

"Thanks, Masters." I pulled out a cigar and laying it on his desk. He nodded his thanks then went back to cussing his papers.

Pat stomped through the door just as I started back up

his face red and his eyes narrowed. I never said a word, just followed, because when he gets the red face, he's extremely pissed. He plopped down at his desk and from the bottom drawer he pulled out a bottle, uncapped it and took a drink. I sat down in the chair beside his desk and waited. Whatever it was that crawled up his ass would come out after the next drink.

"Thanks for leaving me hanging," he snarled.

"So what was it this time?"

That reporter Harley Ames, the bastard, accused me of withholding information from the public. He made the accusation that my department was dirty and I was trying to cover it up," Pat voice rose almost to a yell.

Harley was an old hand at making people mad. He would them up enough so they would slip and spout out information that the police were holding back. Only once did it backfire on him; an interview which landed him in jail 'til the investigation was over. He was still at it though; Harley is a tough old bird.

"Did your boys ever get a line on the waitress?" I asked.

"A couple of witnesses said they saw her go out the back. As the guy put it, *She was a jigglin' and a bouncin' north.*" He capped the bottle and leaned back in his chair. I took a cigar out and lit it, drew in slowly and let the smoke drift out of my mouth.

"She probably thinks she is next on the hit list." I tipped my hat back and blew smoke at the ceiling.

"There's an all points out on her if she hasn't already been gotten to."

"Well let's hope they haven't," I stood and walked to the door. Pat watched as I stopped and turned. "I'm going back to the office for a bit, clear some cobs and see what comes up," I walked on through the door and out of the Station. Yeah, I was going back to the office all right, but not before I had another little set down with Fisk.

CHAPTER 23

It was around ten when I finally walked up to see Fisk. Seems there had been a slight ruckus that had taken place in the bar and I missed it. A couple of fellows had argued and it turned nasty, then deadly. One of the men pulled a knife and cut the other guy up pretty good. Cops were all over the place. The attacker sat in the back of a paddy wagon and screamed his head off about being wrongly accused. Fisk sat on one of the benches outside the bar.

I walked up and sat down beside him. "What's going on?"

"A little knife fight,"

"So who stopped the melee?" I took out a cigar and handed it to him.

"Thanks," He put it between his lips and accepted a light. "Sally."

"Sally? Barfly Sally?" I lit up my own cigar.

"Yeah, seems when the fight broke out and the one guy slashed on the other, blood splattered on Sally. She was lounging with her head down on the bar. In a heartbeat she was off the stool and slammed the guy over the head with a beer mug. Then she cussed a blue streak, told the guy he was gonna pay for the dress. Every time the poor sucker tried to get up she would slam him over the head again. Kelso finally grabbed her and held her down. He took one upside the head also, but not too hard." He flicked ashes. "So what are you doing here?"

"A waitress who works at Cully's, blonde, about 5'3", big boobs. "

"Yeah, I know who she is. Ellen Wade. She came with Bert when Bert opened the restaurant," Fisk said. "I hear his cooking stinks."

"So what was she to Bert, his wife, girlfriend?"

"No, his partner. Rumor has it that before they came here she and Bert were involved in some shady dealings down in Alabama; a blackmail scheme that went sour. The only reason the law probably hasn't caught up with them is because they went by the names of Joe and Millie Barnes."

"Any word on where she might be now?"

"Nope, after that little incident down at the diner, she is in the wind."

I stood and thanked Fisk and was about to leave when the bar's door slammed open. Two uniforms dragged Sally out in cuffs. Sally screamed that she was gonna sue Kelso if he didn't give her the money to clean her dress. I gotta tell you, no amount of money could ever get that dress clean again.

***

The door was slightly open when I got to the office, the lock jimmied. I drew my piece and pushed the door open slowly, the .45 cocked. I got a whiff of perfume and not the kind Shelly wears. Then I heard someone move in my office, the footsteps soft and next to the door.

I stepped up and gripped the door handle, paused, then shoved it open hard. The door connected with a body. A woman's voice cursed. I hit the light switch next to the door and a blonde sat on the floor, her skirt almost up to her waist. Her hand rubbed her shoulder. It was Ellen Wade from the diner.

"Up." She stood and pulled down her skirt, smoothed it, and checked her hair with her hand. I motioned her to one of the chairs in front of my desk and she obliged me by sitting. Her purse was still on the floor so I picked it up and looked through it, just the usual stuff a woman carries so I closed it and tossed it on my desk.

I wondered what was up her sleeve. "What do you want?"

"You gotta help me. They've been looking for me since the hit at Bert's!"

"I figured that," I sat down and rested the .45 on the arm of my chair.

"Look." She leaned closer. Her chest strained against the tight blouse. "I can tell you and that Fed most of what you want to know."

"Okay and I'm sure he will be glad to see you...Millie."

Ellen's mouth dropped open and she started to say something but then shut it quick.

I chuckled and picked up the phone and asked the operator to connect me to Pat's office. When Pat answered, I asked if Trent was there and he said yeah so I told him I had Ellen in my office. He said they would be right down.

After about five minutes, Ellen groaned and looked me straight in the eye. "So how did you find out about the other thing?"

"You mean the blackmail scheme?"

"Yeah."

"A friend of mine told me about it."

"It was all Bert's idea, I mean, he set it up and then he screwed it up."

"How so?"

"He got greedy and that's all I'm gonna say till the cops get here."

"Fair enough."

Pat and Agent Trent walked in about fifteen minutes later. Once they were in the office, I shoved my .45 back home and watched her as Pat and Trent got comfortable.

"Now, Ellen, tell us what you know," Trent ordered.

"Uh-uh." She gave him the eye. "I wanna deal."

"And what deal might that be?"

"Immunity, and the charges dropped on the blackmailing deal down in Alabama."

"That might be a little hard to do since a certain Senator was involved," Trent leaned toward her. "But maybe I can make it go away if you cooperate by giving me names and by telling me everything about what the hell is going on."

"She drew in a deep breath and slowly let it out. "About ten years ago, Ava was sent down here from New York to set up business here. She bought an old house and renovated it, opened up and told the boys in New York that everything was ready."

"Ready for what," Trent cut in.

She glared at him. "I'm getting to that, if you'll stop interrupting me."

I stifled a snicker at the look on Trent's face. She was a tough little number, I had to give her that.

"At first it was dope and hookers, mostly dope. Some of it sold here. Bert and Perkins handled the distribution. The rest shipped out to Kansas, Arkansas and Oklahoma. But then, something came along that made a hell of a lot more money than the dope. Women, especially young women, and the younger the better. It's like an underground railroad. They come up from the southern states, and a few from around here, they are kept at Ava's for a while and then moved out to other locations. They keep 'em doped up so they don't get away."

"Have any of them ever got away?" I asked.

Ellen paused for a moment. Her gaze dropped to the floor. "There was one." Her voice was soft. "A blonde, she'd run off and they would catch her and dope her up. The last time they doped her up a little too much."

I leaned forward on my desk, and kept my voice low. "So they chain her to a chunk of concrete and dump her in the river. Did she have a name?"

"I'm sure, but don't know it."

I grunted and pulled out the picture of the Gates woman then tossed in front of her on the desk.

"Is this the one?" I thumped the picture with my finger.

Ellen picked it up and then laughed as she tossed it back on the desk. "Take a good look at that photo and then think, shamus. You've seen her probably more times than I can count. In fact, there is the same picture in the parlor of her business before a sawbones did some work on her face." She smirked.

I did and that gnawing sensation suddenly ate its way through and I swore under my breath. "Ava," I said softly. That was what I had seen in the house on my visit—another picture of her, the same picture but taken in a different setting. I looked at Pat and he nodded. The prints not so much needed now, except to identify the dead girl. But for some reason my gut told me there was more.

"Becky Gates didn't run away here; she went to New York where she met a certain boss who took a liking to her and set her up in the business, changed her looks and everything. She was his main squeeze, so to speak, and he took good care of her, let me tell you. Then, when they needed a distribution point, he sent her here. When her daddy died, the brothers searched for her. A PI by the name of Herd found her a little quicker than you did. She kind of still resembled the photo they had given him. Herd disappeared and her brothers just figured she had paid him off to leave her alone."

"I remember that," Pat said. "We found the body but never did identify it because it was in the river too long."

"So her brothers knew what she was into?" I asked.

"No, they wanted to find her because of her share of the distillery. You see, dear old daddy put a kink in their way of running the company. In his will, all three had to agree on any changes that were made, especially money-wise, which was where the kink came in. Daddy put the lawyer in charge of any money transactions in his will. The brothers wanted to keep the distillery going and the lawyer wanted them to get rid of it.

Then the accident happened, if it was an accident. Rumor is that the lawyer had ties with Holton and with all the family members gone, he would have full control to sell the distillery and make a hefty profit."

"So they sent this Herd fellow and maybe he found out more than he should," Pat said.

"Maybe the distillery explosion wasn't an accident," I rubbed my chin.

"Yeah," Pat answered.

"Who's Ava's boss?" Trent asked.

I glanced at him and noticed he was a little tense, his eyes narrowed slightly.

She looked at each of us. Fear filled her eyes and her hands trembled slightly.

"Sal Taylor." Once the name was out, she looked as if a weight had been lifted. Trent nodded and scribbled the name in the notebook.

I knew the name. North Side Sal. From what I had heard, he was the main man in the north section of New York and was gaining ground in the south of the city, also. Booze, gambling, wire services. Word was he was soon to be the king of all of it, if the Commission didn't shut him down first. And that looked like it wasn't going to happen.

The white slavery gig Ellen talked was a nasty business, one that would answer a lot of questions for people who had had young girls just disappear without a trace. I leaned forward on my desk and stared straight into Ellen's eyes. A foul stare that told her I meant business.

"There are others connected to this. I suppose those are the ones you don't know."

"That's right," she said. "Only Perkins and Ava knew who the boss here is. Bert nosed around once and got the beating of his life and was told not to be so nosey.

"Bert was in charge of distribution, both of the girls and the money. Those guys sitting around when you first came to visit, those were the delivery boys. The money would come in around the fifteenth of each month, we'd take our cut, then count it out, bundle it, then someone would come pick it up."

"And the delivery boys?' I probed.

"They were paid from another location."

I liked the way she was giving up the information. "Who picked it up?" I just wondered if after she spilled her guts, Trent would keep his part of the bargain.

"Some short, snobby bitch. She never said a word to me, and all she said to Bert was the date of the next delivery."

"So when's the next delivery date?" Pat asked.

"In two weeks. But not to the diner. Bert told me this time the money would be delivered with the girls, and I'd have to go pick it up."

"Why the change?"

"Hell if I know, but he said the bitch told him she would pick me up on the fifteenth and we would go after it. Then she said something funny," Ellen's face went a little pale.

"And that was what?" Trent asked.

"That if Black ever figured out that Ava was Becky then everything would go to hell in a hand basket, especially with the money," Ellen said, her voice almost a whisper.

"Maybe we ought to stake out Ava's," Pat said.

"Maybe." I stood. "What do you think, Trent?"

"Couldn't hurt, but not all of us and not right away," he replied. "We'll wait till the money drop, follow you and the snobby bitch, and then play it from there."

I turned to the coat rack behind my desk and grabbed my slicker as a rumble of thunder shook the building. "You two see to business here." I put the slicker on. "I need to visit a friend."

I handed Pat the key and told him to lock up. When I stepped out into the heat, the air was so heavy it seemed to press wet, damp fingers against my skin. What few people were on the street were taking care of business as fast as they could. Wind whipped down the corridor of Commercial Street, thrashing loose papers and other debris around in the gutters. The wind was hot but damp. The storm rumbled above me.

As I walked toward Kelso's I let what Ellen said mull around in my mind, not about me finding Becky who was Ava, but the money. Was Bert skimming? Was Ellen skimming? Or were they both? Another rumble of thunder cut the air and another gust of wind, cooler this time, sped down Commercial Street, the smell of rain on it. I picked up my pace and hoped I got to Kelso's before the skies decided to take a piss.

CHAPTER 24

The rain started about the time I got halfway to Kelso's. It was late evening so not many people were on the streets. It was a heavy downpour that quickly flooded the streets, overflowing the curbs and running toward the businesses doorways.

I stepped into Kelso's, dripping wet, took off the slicker and shook it in the doorway, folded it over my arm and walked to where Fisk sat, a beer on the table in front of him. I nodded to the Kelso and he nodded back. In a few minutes he brought me an Irish whiskey after I slid into the booth across from Fisk.

"Kill anybody on the way here?" Fisk asked.

"Nope." I sipped the whiskey. "Raining too hard."

"Well, I guess there is always the lull."

I set the whiskey down. "I have a question." I looked Fisk square in the eyes. "Did you know about the white slavery business going on?"

It was the first time I had ever seen a reaction from him.

"No." He met my gaze straight on.

I could see the wheels were turning in his head. No words passed my lips, I just waited.

"But I bet you wanna know more about it."

"If you can find anything out."

"Gonna cost you, Max, more than the palm money you pay me."

"How much?"

"Fifty."

I would have paid a hundred to put the hiatus on this slavery thing, but I didn't want him to know it, he'd try to squeeze me for more. "I can handle that."

"Good, come back later tonight. I'll try to have something for you."

I nodded and stood, downed the rest of the whiskey and held out my hand. Fisk shook it then drew back his hand, looked at it and grinned.

"Little extra." I smiled and walked away.

The rain was still coming down hard. It flooded the streets and washed up over the sidewalk. I noticed it running into some of the business' doorways that were sidewalk level. Al's was one of them.

He was rolling up towels and stuffing them in the doorway. Allie mopped up what was getting through. I motioned to him and he opened the door to let me in. I knew he didn't want to because it would only let more water in, but he did anyway.

"New seals tomorrow and they might not help," he said shaking his head.

I helped him stuff towels, and noticed the rain was letting up and water wasn't gushing in as bad. "Is Shelly upstairs?"

"Oh yeah, she's up there." He had a cockeyed smirk on his face. "Got your iron underwear on?"

"What?"

"Just a warning," he snickered.

Al had moved the three of them into the rooms over his

shop while their house was being fixed. Jack was still in the hospital. I stepped through the doorway and called Shelly's name. She marched out of the small kitchenette and glared at me. Then she crossed the floor in three steps, stopped, and hit me on the arm, hard enough to bring a grunt. She didn't care if she hurt me or not, she just tore into me.

"You asshole! Here I've been worrying myself to death about you, not knowing if you were alive or–"

It was like she couldn't bring herself to say the word *dead.* She started to tear up so I took her into my arms. It felt good when she hugged me back.

"Sorry, Kitten. It probably was a good thing I didn't call or come to see you. They've been getting information somehow." She leaned back and gazed up at me. I wiped the tears out of her eyes. "Things are still pretty dicey so I may not be around as much as you like."

"When is it gonna be over, Max?"

"Soon, I hope, real soon."

I left Al's around ten that evening. The rain had stopped, but the air was drenched in moisture. I walked the short distance to Kelso's, watching the street for cars that might suddenly come to life. Nothing happened.

I stepped in the door and looked around. The regular crowd was still there, but I notice some figures in the back nestled at a table in the darkness. Three of them.

Kelso slightly shifted his eyes toward the shadows. I walked on, but kept a close watch on the table out of the corner of my eye. One of them leaned over and talked to the other next to him. That one shook his head.

Fisk sat in his booth. He nodded a greeting and cut his eyes in the same direction Kelso had. I quietly let him know I'd already been warned. "So what is the scoop?"

Fisk leaned forward a little on the table. "Those three are supposed to be Feds."

"Is that so?" I glanced over at them, "What about the other thing you were gonna find out about?"

"A dead end. Every time I ask around, the well dries up."

"I wonder if Trent—"

"Nada. These boys are working for the one who is in charge of all this, that I am sure of. They came in here asking a lot of questions about you. If they worked for Trent they would already be informed. Eddie, remember him?"

"Sure."

"They asked him about you and he told them to buzz off. They told him that they could take him in or he could answer their questions here. He told them what they could do with themselves and they hauled him out. He hasn't been back. I did get something that might help."

He sat back away from the table and I felt his hand tap my knee. I slid my hand off the table and reached under it as he slipped me piece of paper. I leaned back and shoved it in my coat pocket.

"That phone number was all I could get. I was told if you leaned on this person hard enough you might get them to talk."

"Max Black?" a voice said beside me.

I looked up and the three from the shadows stood beside us. The room suddenly got quiet as a tomb. The man flashed his badge quick and then slipped it back in his coat pocket.

"Didn't see that ID real clear, partner. Mind if I see it again?"

He leaned on the table and his hand went in and came out with a .38 snub nose, the pistol an inch from my chest.

"How is this for ID? Just get up and come with us." The others backed toward the door, coats unbuttoned and ready to grab.

"Hey." Fisk sat up straight in the booth. "What about my money!"

The man glanced at the little man. "Shut up, wop."

Fisk frowned and looked at me. "Did he just call me a wop?"

I saw a sparkle in him eye. "Yeah, he did." I braced myself for what was going to happen.

It was over in three seconds. Fisk's hand came up and down, the sap in his hand smacked the gun hand of the, so-called, Fed hard. He howled as his wrist bones broke. I swung out of the booth; drew my feet up, planted them in his chest and knocked him across the room.

Kelso had already unloaded his sawed off at the two who were trying to dig their guns out from under their coats; one shell each. He had a good aim.

I stood and walked over to the one still alive. Fisk stepped on his hand and he screamed. I bent down and liberated the leather folder he had in his coat pocket. Just a kid's fake Fed badge but it looked real if it was flashed fast enough.

"Well, Mr. Fed, least they let you live," I said, rising. Kelso set the phone on the bar so I could call Pat. Fisk put pressure on the fake Fed's hand if he even flinched.

CHAPTER 25

The sun heated the streets again the next morning. The water, where it wasn't standing in puddles, had dried up and the puddles followed a close second. The heat had built up again outside, and my office felt it.

My fan was turning. The air from it remained hot and humid, but it was moving air and helped a little. I leaned back in my chair and propped my feet up. I mulled over the past few days events and tried to make sense of what happened.

Ellen said Sal Taylor was running the show; he had changed. Sal liked kids alright, but not in that way. I heard a story one time where one of his hoods had been keeping a fourteen year old girl in his apartment and Sal had found out. A few days later, said hood was found in an alley, dead, and his boys missing. No, I didn't believe Sal was running this. Somebody else was in charge besides Ava; somebody who had the authority to keep me, and anybody else in their way, watched.

Trent told us the three in Kelso's had at one time been Feds but were deep into the New York bunch, and had warrants out on them. If anything, they were under orders from the one running this show to keep track of anyone getting close.

Or so Trent said. After his interview with Ellen, I wasn't so sure if he was getting information to end this case or if he was getting information to see what she knew. I felt like he was seeing if she knew who the main guys were. Don't think I didn't catch the way his eyes narrowed and his body tensed when she was asked.

Perkins had referred to the other person as his partner and boss. The only other that would remotely come close to that was Carlton. But I wondered if maybe Carlton was just a flunky. I set my feet back on the floor from my desk top and wondered. Carlton was in the know about most of the things that went on where the police were concerned, but could he have connections in the Fed department?

Could Trent be his connection? If he was, he played us all for a bunch of fools. For some reason I doubted that, but wasn't dismissing it either. Although he was one of the little guys, I didn't doubt Carlton's connection in this. But who was getting the info to the hoods? Who was keeping track of me?

I swiveled my chair, got up, and went out to the front of the office. The clouds gathered again. The sun slowly faded as I left the office and locked up. I turned and started to take a step. Thunder boomed and I saw what I thought was a flash of light. Then the world fell on me.

***

"Max, Max buddy, come on Max!"

I thought the booming was thunder but it wasn't. Someone's voice boomed in my head. I tried to sit up and was suddenly sick to my stomach, so I lay back. The feeling subsided. Shelly knelt beside me, her face a smear of mascara and make up. Behind her stood Fisk.

A shotgun rested over his shoulder, the stock busted off. Al was on the other side of me, covering me with a slicker. His clothes were soaked.

"We need to get you inside, buddy," Fisk said.

I nodded and tried to sit up again. This time the world spun, but no sick stomach. Al and Fisk grabbed me under the arms and pulled me into my office. My head pounded and my feet did't want to work. Shelly grabbed her chair and they parked me in it. I grinned at her and she smiled back. Something ran down the side of my head. I wiped at it and my hand came back red. Definitely not rain water.

I felt Shelly's hands working on me, a towel pressed against the side of my head. Her face swam in and out of focus.

Al ran to the door and then back. "Where the hell is that damned ambulance!" He went back to the door.

"They will be here Al, just stay calm."

That was Fisk. He sounded like he was in a tunnel; his voice echoed. His face appeared in front of me. He talked to Shelly, telling her to put pressure on it, even if it hurt me. She was back again, this time her tears splashed down on me like the rain. I smiled and reached up and touched her cheek. Then there was blackness.

CHAPTER 26

I woke to the smell of antiseptic, the sound of nurse's shoes squeaking, and a doctor flashed a penlight in my eyes. He grinned when I told him to knock it off unless he was looking to see into the depths of my soul.

"Well good to see you're alive," he said.

I tried to sit up and remembered the sick feeling I had gotten before. I eased up and nothing happened. I eased up some more and my head began to spin, so I stopped.

"What happened?" I croaked. My Kitten was beside me then, with a glass of water in her hand and a straw touching my lips. Her face was drawn, her eyes red.

"They shot you, Max." She was on the verge of tears.

"Or tried to!" The Doc took her by the shoulders and set her in the chair by my bed. "You need to rest. Let me talk to Max, okay?"

She nodded and pulled out a well-used hanky and dried her eyes.

"Well, like she said, you were shot. The bullet grazed your head. Then they tried to finish the job by beating you. Your friends saved you from getting killed." He checked the bandage on my head. I winced and he smiled then leaned in close and looked at my eyes again with the light.

"Better take good care of that one," he said in a low voice, nodding toward Shelly. "You have been out three days and she has been right here."

"Yeah, I plan on it," I croaked in as soft a whisper as I could.

He smiled and straightened back up. "I pronounce you better, but not by much."

"Thanks, I think."

Shelly stood and the doc stepped back. She gave him a questioning look and he rolled his eyes. "Yes you can hug him. Just don't break anything else."

He was laughing when he left. Shelly laid on my chest and I put a hand on her head and patted her hair.

"I thought you were dead when I saw you," she said, sniffing, "You were bleeding all over the place!"

Pushing her back, I looked at her swollen eyes. "Easy, Kitten, don't cry so much, you're gonna get sick."

I let her lay her head back on my chest, sniffing tears and hugging my middle. Al came in after a while and I motioned for him to take her. I had been holding her up to keep her from falling into the floor. She had gone to sleep on my chest. Al pulled her back easy, whispered in her ear as he sat her in the chair and covered her with a blanket. I looked over at her. She sure was pretty.

Al stepped toward the bed. "You had us damned scared, Max."

"What exactly happened?" I reached for the water again. Al handed it to me then sat on the edge of my bed.

"They jumped you when you left the office. Fisk was coming out of Kelso's and saw them rush you. I guess he yelled and you started to turn when one of them hit you with a sap. He said he could hear the crack of your head being hit, all the way from Kelso's."

"How many?"

"Four. Fisk yelled for Kelso to bring the trench gun and he tore off down the street. He saw a flash and heard a report, then he was on them. Kelso came up about then and unloaded both barrels. Almost cut one of them in half. Then he used the stock like a club. By the way, he says you owe him a shotgun."

I laughed and that was the wrong thing to do. It hurt like hell.

"Those still standing scattered when they heard the cops coming. Fisk got one last lick in; shot one of them in the back with one of their own guns. Kelso kicked your door in, he says he'll pay for the damages, then he called me. Shelly answered the phone and was out the door running. I yelled but she just kept going. I tore out after her and well...."

I nodded which was not a good thing to do either.

"You almost bought it this time, Max. It was really close." He gripped my shoulder.

"Yeah, I guess it was at that." I kind of realized my mortality at that point.

"You get some rest. We'll talk more in the morning." Al stood, checked on Shelly then was out the door.

CHAPTER 27

Things sometimes come together after a guy almost gets his head caved in. While Shelly slept, I closed my eyes and let my mind drift, bits and pieces of the beating swam in and out of focus. I remembered a scuffing of leather on concrete, a voice yelled, my hand reached for my .45 as I fell.

Fists and feet pounded and kicked, a gun barrel slammed up side my head and my hand grabbed it, pushing it aside as it went off. More fists, a hand gripped my .45. I remembered pulling the trigger and the .45 going off; a grunt as the slide kicked back, the smell of burnt powder and flesh as someone cussed and ran. That was it, nothing after that.

There was a face just before I pulled the trigger, but it swam in and out of focus, too. I tried till my head pounded to remember. Then I let it go and drifted off to sleep.

Trent and Pat came in while Al took Shelly out to get something to eat. She didn't want to leave but I told her to get. Go enjoy the heat, I ain't going anywhere soon." She pouted but she left.

I told Pat and Trent what I had remembered. Both listened and took notes. When I finished, I asked Pat if I could speak to Trent alone. He eyed me for a moment and then left the room.

Trent put his pen behind his ear. "I guess this is where you tell me you suspect me of being one of the bad guys?"

"No," I lied. "But I do believe you know more than you are telling us."

He sat quietly for a moment, ran his hand over the stubble on his chin, then flipped his notepad shut and slipped it in his coat pocket. I tensed and he laughed.

"Easy, Max," He pulled out a pack of cigarettes and wobbled one out. He offered one to me and I shook my head no. "You are right, I have been keeping some things back, but there was a reason."

"And that is?"

He lit the cigarette and drew deep, letting the smoke drift out as he spoke. "We have known about the activity going on in Springfield for a while now. One of our plants, a little blonde haired vixen by the name of Elsa, is working for Ava .She watched from the doorway when you showed Ava the picture. You have a good eye, Max, so she was trying to get you out before you saw the later picture of Ava on the wall."

I nodded. She had been talkative and kept my attention. She had the right tools to keep me occupied.

"So why haven't you busted the bunch yet?" I asked, sitting up some.

"We want the whole, Max, not just a part. We raid them now, they will just move the operation like they have before."

"Before?"

"Yes, like I said, this has been going on for a long time. The last agents moved too fast in St. Louis and they got only the underlings, not the main honchos. This time we will get them all!"

"Including Sal?"

"Including Sal."

I nodded and Trent smiled, then stubbed out the cigarette in the ashtray. He stood and held out his hand. I shook it and his smile widened.

"Get well, Max." He walked toward the door. "You don't want to miss the party two weeks from now."

He saluted me and stepped out the door. Shelly stepping back in with something in that big hand bag she carries. I sniffed the air and grinned, not realizing how hungry I was.

"Benny sends his compliments." She took one of his famous burgers out and laid it on that table they roll in front of you when they feed you that God awful stuff they cook in hospitals. I devoured the whole thing before they could catch me.

CHAPTER 28

They let me out of the hospital and I laid low for a while. Shelly gave me hell if she thought I was trying to sneak away to the office.

Some guys wouldn't like that very much. Me, I thought it was just fine. Hell, she loved me and that's what women do when the one they love almost bites the bullet. But it can get sort of irritating, if you know what I mean.

After about a week and a doctor's visit, he told her to let me get around some and that "some" was down to the Station where Pat and Trent were holding Bert.

He looked about as bad as I did. His face still healed from the glass cuts, his arms sported bandage where they had picked out pellets.

He had told Pat and Trent earlier he had received a call from the boss man a couple of hours before Tony showed up. The deliveries were to be made on the last day of the month, four days from now and the package would be ready for Ellen to pick it up.

When I went with them to talk to him, he told me the same thing. "Package?"

"Yeah, Ellen is to pick up the money."

"You know of any reason why they changed the money delivery?"

Bert shrugged and ducked his head.

"How much is usually in the bag, Bert?"

"Anywhere between eight and ten thousand."

"And did you help her count it?"

"No, she did it herself."

"Always by herself?"

"Yeah, hey, what the hell are you getting at?"

Bert gave me the eye as if I was crazy. I motioned for Trent to step outside with me. "You thinking what I'm thinking?"

'Uh-huh," Trent said nodding. "She was the one skimming. She is in a holding cell at the federal building. Let's get her back down here and see what happens."

"Okay, in the meantime, I want to talk to Bert some more."

Trent agreed and went to one of the desks and picked up the phone.

I stepped back into the room. "Say, Bert. How long you and Ellen been working this deal?"

"We started this year."

I picked up a chair and turned it around backwards, sat down then leaned on the back. "And she always counted the money?"

"She did, took out our cut, then the rest was picked up by a short bitch who acted like she was better than us."

"So you trusted her to do it right?"

"Again, What the hell are you getting at?"

"Well, I believe she was skimming."

"Damn!" Bert leaned forward and rubbed his face with his hands. He drew in a deep breath and let it out slow. "I knew I should have left that bitch down in Alabama."

"Why's that?"

"She was the reason we had to leave. She got greedy

and damned near got us killed!"

"She told us you were the one who got greedy."

"Bullshit. I would have been happy with the ten thousand they were gonna pay us. She went behind my back and tried to up the ante to twenty. They agreed and we set up a pick up point. Only the pickup point was a set up.

"We sent a kid for the money and they nabbed him. The kid squealed like a pig, so we got the hell out of Dodge. Shit!"

I stood and stepped out of the room. The cop standing watch looked at me and I tilted my head in acknowledgment that we were done with the man.

Bert went back to his cell knowing that she was the one who damned near got him killed because of her greed. It's just like Samson said, the boss always gets a little pissed when his crew steals from him, this one included.

Trent pulled Ellen in. Her eyes darted back and forth as Trent waltzed her down to the interrogation room. I was in Pat's office chewing the fat with him when she arrived so we went down to join them.

"Ok, Ellen," Trent leaned back in his chair. "Seems you have a few holes in the story you told us."

"Holes?" she said, her voice cracking just a bit.

"Yeah, like you counting the money," Trent leaned forward. His eyes locked with hers. "You sure you didn't short the boss a little?"

She sat silent for a moment then let out a laugh, her eyes suddenly narrowing. "You know how much we got for the risk we were taking? Two hundred damned dollars a month, and the drivers got less! Hell, there was over ten grand in that case. You damned right I took some of it, about a grand worth each time!"

"Whoa, whoa, you told us you were paid five hundred," Trent said.

"Yeah I did, but I figured I deserved more than that. Bert, well, if he got burned down because of it I'd just disappear and that would be that," she said with a wicked smile, "I just didn't figure it would be so soon."

"So you planned on flying the coop that day?" Trent asked.

"Yeah, I was. I planned on being long gone before they did what they did. I forgot he wore that damned vest part of the time. He called it insurance."

"Where did he get the vest?" Trent kept interrogating.

"Hell, I don't know," Ellen glared at him. "He just wore it one day!"

I shook my head. She was a cold dame, cold and greedy. If Bert had gotten killed, she would be on her way west, a lot richer. Until they figured out it wasn't Bert who had stiffed them.

Pat stepped forward. "This woman who came and picked up the money, how was she dressed?"

"Like I told you before, a business suit, usually gray or brown; short, brown hair cut in a pageboy with bangs. She wears these glasses that magnify her eyes which are brown. I told you this shit before."

Trent grinned and leaned forward onto the table. "Was she the one who always showed up?"

"Yes."

I left her with Trent and Pat and I stepped out of the room. I leaned against the door and rubbed my temple. We had all the info, but now how to use it. Bert was supposed to be dead and I figured they already knew he had survived. On the other hand, Ellen had been kept on ice. None of us had told either of the high command where she was or that we had talked with her. I had an idea. Trent would probably go along with it. Whether Ellen would, would be another story.

When they came out and Ellen was taken back to the Federal Building, we went back to Pat's office and I spilled the plan to them.

"She'll face jail time if she doesn't agree," Trent said

after I filled him in. "She will be prosecuted to the full extent and once she gets inside, well..."

"And if she agrees?" I asked.

"Then we offer her the immunity she asked for before."

Pat groaned and shook his head. I smiled and thought to myself, *if they don't get her first.*

***

She wasn't gonna agree until Trent said that he would also *stick* the charge of blackmail, along with premeditated murder, for setting Bert and the other guy up for the kill.

Once she and Trent were in agreement, we set up the plan. The next morning when she went in to work, Bert's second in command, a fellow by the name of Nick, took her in the back, and after ten minutes came back out, turned the closed sign around and locked the door. I looked at Trent but he was already out of the car moving toward the diner.

We both entered the alley at the same time, one against each wall. We moved toward a window that was opened just a crack. Muffled voices came from inside. Next to the window there was a door and through the frosted glass I could see people. Ellen was doing a fine job of denying knowing anything about the money. She told them Bert had been the one who had tended to that. She had only counted it and then turned it over to Bert.

They didn't buy it. Someone said she was lying and there was a dull smack. Ellen cursed.

"The son of a bitch was stupid for crossing you guys," she said in a tense voice.

"I bet," the man said. "Where've you been?"

"Hiding out. Hell, I was scared. Wouldn't you be?"

"Yeah, guess I would be. Ok, here's the deal, a car will come and pick you up, and take you to pick up the money. Bring it back here. Nick will watch while you do the count.

After that, we'll decide what to do with you."

There was silence for a couple beats. Then there was a laugh. The voice sounded funny as if the person had a mouth full of something.

"Don't worry Ellen, you do what you're told and we might, just might, let you live."

I heard a door open and close, so I moved back to the mouth of the alley and peeked around. I only caught a glimpse of a man as he walked around the corner of the diner. I ducked back in and motioned to Trent. He came over with a questioning look on his face. I looked back around and the guy had already disappeared. I shook my head and we both left the alley before someone spotted us and got wise.

CHAPTER 29

Ellen was watched for the next couple of days, but after that, she had old Nicky boy twirled around her finger. The day before the drop, Nicky got a phone call; he listened for a moment then hung up. Called Ellen into the kitchen and gave her the dope.

She told us she, and the uptown bitch, would go at midnight. She would make the pickup and they would drive back here, and he would take care of the money. That was when they would decide if she was still of use, or not.

"Probably not," Pat lit up a cigar. He had borrowed one from me and decided it was better than a cigarette; it lasted longer. "She knows it, too. She said she was calling from a phone booth in the Landmark Building."

"Yeah," Trent said, "they'll probably do away with her coming back. The road they take passes right by the river."

"Pop her, dump her in the river, and drive back. Couple of weeks later she shows up downstream, a slug between her eyes." I said.

"Be that as it may," Trent piped in. "We need to see that it doesn't happen."

I nodded and stood up, told them I had a bathing beauty to visit, and left.

I felt better, but work always does that for me, especially when a case is beginning to wind down. I walked into Al's and up the stairs. Shelly sat on the couch listening to some music. I pulled off my hat and jacket and hung them on the peg by the door, and sat down beside her. "What, no smothering me in kisses anymore?"

"Allie says I should have more control of myself," she said, glancing at the kitchenette.

"Oh, so she thinks you kiss me too much?" I asked.

"That and other things," she said, giving me an impish grin.

"What do you think?"

"I think the hell with it!" she said. She grabbed me around the neck and kissed me long and sweet. When I looked up, Allie stood in the kitchenette shaking her head and smiling.

After dinner, I went down to the shop and picked out a good cigar, stepped outside and lit up. The night air was still humid and hot, but tolerable. As I smoked, I thought back on the voice in the diner and the person it belonged to. It had sounded like no one I knew, but the voice was muffled, as if he were speaking around a mouth full of cotton. And maybe he had been speaking around a mouth full of cotton.

I remembered a case I worked a few years back, a kidnapping where the phone calls sounded like that. It was one way to disguise a voice, but not the best.

And the clothes I got a glimpse of. Tailored clothes, but tailored to a small frame. Carlton wasn't a small man so it wasn't him. Ellen said the woman who came to pick up the valise was small. I smiled and flicked off the ash of my cigar, then chuckled and watched the street grow dark. Another storm built just as it was getting twilight.

Al had come down to lock the door to the shop. I

stubbed out the cigar and tossed it in the gutter. I walked back in as a flicker of lighting lanced across the sky and a second later, thunder boomed. I hoped this one broke the heat, but hope and happening are two different things.

***

"That voice we heard yesterday." I tossed my coat on a chair in my office. "I remember a case one time where a kidnapper disguised his voice by stuffing his cheeks with cotton; made him talk different."

"I've heard of that." Trent met me just as I got there. Both of us sweated in the humid, morning heat. "And talking a little lower or higher would help also."

"In this case, probably a little lower," I sat down and leaning back in my old swivel chair. "The person I saw going around the corner of the diner? I suspect wasn't a male."

"How could you tell?"

"The clothes weren't cut right and the person walked with a smaller stride."

"Could have been a small man?"

"Nope, the clothes were cut to try and hide the form, but they didn't do it. Besides, now that I think about it, the sway of the hips gave it away. Too much swing."

"So who, then?"

I didn't want to give it up yet. "I'd guess, but I think I'll wait."

Trent stayed for a few more minutes and then left. I leaned back farther in the chair and closed my eyes for a moment. I could have told him who I thought was the mystery person, but like I said, I wanted to wait and see if my guess was right. If that was the case, then we would be just that much closer to snagging the head man. I sat up quickly, swore under my breath. What if a woman was the brains?

I was about to call Pat when Shelly stepped in. I kissed her, then stood. "Kitten, where would a woman go to have a suit tailored to try to hide her curves?"

"Hiram Smith," she said with a questioning look. "Why, Max?"

The same tailor popping into my mind. "Oh, just a little thought I had last night. Do what you gotta do and I'll see you back to Al's. I need to go talk to Hiram."

She went back out to her desk as I picked up the phone to call Pat.

CHAPTER 30

I dropped by Hiram's shop, a little hole in the wall place between the Paramount Theater and Barth's. The little guy told me, yes, he did tailor suits for women, but not many. The only ones he had done recently were for a woman who worked for the D.A., and another lady who he had no idea what she did.

Hiram asked what it was all about and I told him not to concern himself with it, just a routine check. I left, and the minute I was out the door, I stopped and lit a cigar. I glanced back through his window and saw him on the phone. I grinned and headed to see Pat.

It was late afternoon when I got to the Station. Pat sat at his desk, the file I had asked him for was in front of him.

Trent was in his office when I got there, sitting on the couch, smoking a cigarette. I plopped down in the chair by Pat's desk and reached for the file. I watched Trent out of the corner of my eye when I said the name written on it. Trent hesitated for a second when he drew on the cigarette; his eyes cut toward me.

I opened the folder and read for a few minutes, one eye

on Trent and the other on the file.

"You wanna let us in on the secret?" Pat said, finally.

"Hiram Smith, before he came here, was a tailor in New York," I closed the folder. "Having learned his trade in the old country, he was very good. So good that a lot of the hoods in New York visited him to get their suits tailored by him. One of those hoods was Sal Taylor."

Pat just nodded but Trent paused, the cigarette almost to his lips as he stared at me. I continued. "It appears that Hiram did a lot of work for Sal and his boys; in fact, he did more than just tailor suits. He seems to have been tangled up in a little incident that involved a wire service," I said. "Said wire service was run by a couple of sour Feds, the same Feds that I had a tussle with down at Kelso's."

Trent leaned forward and crushed out his smoke in the ashtray on Pat's desk. He probably didn't think I'd notice, but the corner of his mouth had a slight tick in it.

"It seems there was another fellow involved also, this one being the boss of the wire service. The two Feds collection men, hassled fellows who owed money on their bets. When the Feds got enough evidence to take the wire service down, Hiram and his buddies were gone, so all they got was the wire service people. Am I right, Trent?"

"Correct." Trent leaned back. "He's been on our list of those to keep an eye on since he got here."

"Then why not nail him here?" Pat asked.

"Not so easy. I was gonna do just that and was told not to, just to keep him under surveillance." Trent shrugged. "So what's this got to do with the woman, if it is a woman?"

"Well, I paid Hiram a little visit, asked him if he could alter my jackets to hide the bulge under my arm better. He checked things out and said he could. While he was doing that, we chatted for a bit and I asked him if any women ever came to him for alterations. He told me there was one who came in every so often. A short woman who told him she couldn't get clothes to fit her. He said she worked in city hall for a big shot lawyer."

Pat chimed in. "Carlton."

Trent cleared his throat. "I had another talk with Bert. He told me a woman always called him and gave him the date for the pickups. This last time it was a man, or it sounded like a man,"

"Let's get Carlton down here," Pat said. "See if he involved or not."

"I bet you a fin he does." I said, grinning.

Pat picked up the phone "You're on."

***

District Attorney Carlton is a tall man, over six feet tall, lanky but muscular in a toned sort of way. His hair wavy brown, his face long, coming to a point at his chin. The job had begun to take a toll on his face. Deep lines showed in the corner of his eyes and mouth. He owned a horse ranch and the summer sun had browned his skin the color of old leather. Gray eyes flashed when he looked at you, and a fine set of teeth accompanied them, pearly and political.

"So," he said, flashing those pearly whites and shaking everyone's hands, "What is it you wanted to talk to me about?"

"How many women you have working in your office, Carlton?" I asked.

He looked at me, his eyes narrowing as he thought about it. "About six, why?"

"Is one of them a skinny little woman, tailored suits, and brown hair cut in a pageboy style with bangs?" Trent asked.

He looked at Trent questioningly. "Sounds like you're talking about Marissa."

I asked the next question. "She have access to the

communiqués coming in and going out of your office

"Well, yes, she is the head secretary and takes care of all my messages. What is this all about?"

I told him what we suspected and his mouth dropped open and he muttered words I never thought I would hear him say.

"How long has she been with you?" Trent asked.

"Ten years. I hired her right after she graduated college."

I kept an eye on him. "She does errands for you?"

"Yes, she does."

"Any in the downtown area?"

"From time to time. Why?"

I pushed forward. "We suspect she has been doing some payoff pickups for a certain fellow by the name of Sal. You wouldn't know anything about that, would you?"

"No, no I don't."

He was getting nervous, picking at the crease in his slacks as he looked from me, to Pat then Trent. "Anything else?" He started to stand up. I reached over, put a hand on his shoulder, and pushed gently back down in the chair.

"You seem a little nervous, Carlton, never seen you like that before."

"Oh, I have my moments, Max." He looked at me with a weak smile.

"Having one now?"

His face grew dark for just a second and I thought he was going to say no, Then took in a deep breath and let it out slow. "Maybe it's time. Lord knows I have tried to keep this hidden for a long time."

Trent leaned toward Carlton. "And what's *this*?"

"Well," he took another deep breath, "about eight years ago, I was looking for a file on a case that was going to court. Marissa was out to lunch, so I went to her desk and rummaged around. In one of her file draws I found a valise. It was heavy, and when I opened it, it was full of money. I put it back, took it out again and carried it into my office. Why, I don't have a clue, but I counted it and there was a little over six thousand dollars in it!

"When she came back, I called her into my office and explained what I was looking for and what I found. She didn't stutter and make excuses. She came around my desk, leaned over as if she was about to tell me something and the next thing I knew I had a straight razor at my throat!

"She told me I shouldn't have been so nosy. Said I had a choice, either listen to what she had to say, or find myself out of a job and in the pen with all the scum I had sent there. It was an election year, gentleman, and she said she had some very revealing photos to show me. Then she stepped back and left the office.

"Why I didn't stop her or call for the cops while she was gone, I don't know, I guess I was just dumbfounded that this little lady could be capable of what she had just done. I sat there till she came back and tossed a manila envelope on my desk."

He paused, took another deep breath. "Yes, she did have the photos she said she had, how she got them was probably from that whore, Ava, and yes, I have been there on occasion. Sorry if that sullies my reputation for you."

Pat tapped his desk with a pencil. "Keep talking."

"Our deal was, she would launder the money through city accounts," he continued. "I would keep my mouth shut and the pictures would stay invisible."

"So she is the one behind this then, the white slavery?" I asked. He sweated big time. I had never seen Carlton sweat like that before.

"Yes, her and Ava." He took out a handkerchief and wiped his face.

Trent motioned for me to step back so he could talk to me.

"You buying this?" he asked in a low voice.

"Yeah, for now, why?"

"For one thing, looks like the county auditor would have caught the money going through."

"Unless he's involved, or blackmailed like Carlton."

"I'm gonna do some checking, see what I can find out," Trent said. "See what else you can get out of him, and let me know." He turned and walked out the door.

I watched him walk away and in my mind I wondered why he hadn't stayed. I mean, I have known some agents, and most of them would have grilled Carlton until he broke with more information, not rushed off to check on something.

I turned back and watched Carlton and Pat talk. Pat was still asking questions and Carlton was still sweating. Maybe there was something to what Trent said. I walked back in, sat down, and listened. It felt as if Carlton was holding something back with each answer.

Pat gave him a choice. "Help us clean this up and things we'll try to keep everything under wraps so your family doesn't find out. Refuse and your career will end, as will your reputation."

He chose to help. I nodded, told him to go back and we would be in contact with him. Pat took him back to his office, as I mulled over whether it was worth it.

CHAPTER 31

The pickup was at midnight.

Ellen said that they would be in a dark green Chevy Sedan. Trent and I watched from our parking spot in front of the Colonial in a black Ford Coupe. Just us. Pat was keeping an eye on Carlton just in case he was lying to us.

At eleven thirty the Chevy pulled up to the diner and Nicky and Ellen came out. The driver wore a fedora, and even with the street light shining right on them, I couldn't make out who was under the hat.

Nick opened the door for Ellen, she got into the passenger then he shut it and stepped back onto the sidewalk. The car pulled out, made a left onto Jefferson and headed south to the country. We stayed a few cars behind as the houses got fewer and the lights less. Trent switched off the lights and drove. The only thing keeping us out of the ditches was the full moon.

We made a left on a dirt road they call the River Road. Moonlight shone off the river, the surface looked silvery black. A lot of kids came out here to park and hopefully get lucky; spots in the brush, where they'd parked over the years, visible in the moonlight. There was no one there since it was midweek, which was good, because if it came down to gun play, the less the better.

We still kept our distance and soon they were pulling into Ava's back drive. Trent found a short drive along the road and backed into it. He pulled far enough back so that when the lights of any other car came by they wouldn't see us. As he backed up, scratching sounds came from the rear until he stopped.

"Herb's gonna be real happy with me," Trent said and chuckled.

"Who?" I jerked my head toward him.

"Herb, the guy who takes care of the Fed Fleet. A dozen cars, and he keeps them in tip top order. Scratches are one of his pet peeves. I have seen him almost cry."

There was nervousness in Trent's voice. His eyes darted from me to the road, one finger tapped on the steering wheel.

He let the words dwindle as the sedan's head lights came into view. We watched as the car pulled up the slight hill and the driver shifted. The car gained speed when it hit the flat road. Trent waited a couple of minutes and started the Ford, eased out of our hiding place and pulled his pistol out as he did.

The branches on the back fenders made the metal squeal. A cold chill ran up my back. My own hand reached under my coat and pulled lose my .45. My gut twisted as my finger hooked the trigger and my thumb got ready on the hammer.

"Yep, he is gonna be pissed!" Trent chuckled again as the taillights of the Chevy grew dimmer in the distance. We drove with the lights off and I rolled down my window. The smell of the James River touched my nose. I kept one eye on Trent and one on the car. We started around a curve and suddenly Trent slowed, the taillights of the Chevy a few feet ahead. We stopped and sat for a moment. The sounds of two people arguing filled the night air. Suddenly two shots echoed loud in the moonlit countryside.

I was out first, my piece came out from under my coat and my thumb pulled back the hammer. I kept to the shadows. Trent passed through a patch of moonlight and there was another shot, this one kicking dust up on his left side. He dove for the ground and ate dirt. Another shot and the car jumped forward, tires kicking out gravel. I fired twice, one slug pounded the trunk lid, knocking it open as the car sped off. The other whined off into thin air.

"Trent!" I yelled as I ran down the road.

"Yeah, good here!" He spat. Guess he did eat some dirt.

There were two figures on the side of the road. I swore as I reached for my flash and remembered I had left it in the car. Trent ran up beside me. His light flashed on. Two of them lay there. One was dressed like a man, but wasn't. A .45 slug had entered her back and tore a hole in her chest. Marissa's eyes stared. The other was Ellen. She had been shot through the neck. I knelt beside her and felt for a pulse. She gasped and grabbed my hand.

"Jesus." Trent shined the flashlight on Ellen. "I'll go get the car."

"Too...late..." Ellen coughed and trickle of blood ran from the corner of her mouth.

"Easy, lady." I knelt beside her.

She didn't answer. As I watched, the life faded from her eyes, replaced by stone cold moonlight.

CHAPTER 32

We found the car in one of the downtown lots, parked there in the night when the attendant wasn't on duty. Trent's people fingerprinted the vehicle but found nothing; most of the prints too smudged to do any good.

The front seat was bloody from where whoever was in the back had blasted Marissa. My bullet hole was in the trunk lid. A couple inches over to the right it would have found a home in the driver as they were making tracks.

I stood looking down at where the bullet had come through the seat and hit the dash, but it hadn't punched through, only a dent showed in the dash. I fished around in the seat for a bit, in between the back of the seat and under it. If the slug had of ricocheted off the dash it should be in the car somewhere.

It wasn't in the car. I mentioned this to Trent and Pat both. We went over the car with a fine tooth comb again; still no slug.

"You think maybe..." Trent said, looking at me. I nodded.

"It has happened. Few years back, a fellow in St. Louis

was in a gun fight with the cops at a construction site. One of the cops fired at him and he ducked, the slug hit a piece of steel and bounced back, hit him in the back of the head and killed him," I said.

"So it could have bounced off the dash and…" Trent sat in the car, pointed at the dash and the dent. Pat and I followed the path of his arm.

I could see where he was going with this. "Either hit them in the shoulder or, hit them in the chest and lodged there under the skin, maybe. Depends on how many clothes they had on."

Both men nodded as I stood, leaned against the car, pulled out a cigar and lit it. How many clothes, I thought to myself, how many clothes?

***

Allie had made me a bed on the sofa, a big green job with plush cushions and padded arms. I told them I could sleep in the upstairs above my office, but Shelly wouldn't have it.

As for sleeping with her, well, that was a no go all the way around, so I opted for the couch, no matter how frustrated it made me. Shelly and I hadn't been together for a while now, and I was beginning to get a little randy. She was too, more her than me.

I let things roll around in my mind while I looked the room over in the dark. The apartment was a nice one with a living room, kitchenette and two bedrooms. Allie had done wonders with the place. The last time I was up here the room was dust, cobwebs and broken furniture.

Across from me sat a long and narrow table made of walnut, the legs carved in those clawed feet that most women are nuts about nowadays. On top of it sat a silver tea set. Al told me it had been in Allie's family for generations, handed down from mother to daughter, and so forth.

On either side of it sat candles in decorative holders, silver colored candlesticks completing the look. On either side of the table were the doors to the bedrooms, the one on the left Al and Allie's, the one on the right Shelly's. Neither room had much in it but a dresser with mirror, a small closet, and a bed. Al told me that those rooms had held the bookies, this room for the accountants and money counters.

The downstairs was for the locals who came in, passed bets off to a fellow that wasn't a barber, and his partner took them upstairs to be placed. I asked him why they did it backwards and he said they had tapped into the phones on the back side of the building without the phone companies consent. One operator in cahoots with them patched their calls through.

That was how they got caught. The phone people got wise somehow, called in the feds and they nailed them. I stood up and walked to the kitchen and took a Coca-Cola from the icebox, popped the cap and swallowed half before I went back to the sofa.

The floor was uneven as I walked across it. Allie had thrown down some rugs to keep a person from getting splinters when they were in their bare feet.

I sat down and looked out the window; it was open because the air conditioning vent to the upstairs was not connected. Something Al was still trying to get fixed.

The moon was full tonight, the main street bathed in its silvery glow. Black shadows pooled beneath the awnings of the businesses, light and dark ending and beginning in a definite line. I was still rolling it over in my mind about the slug. As I watched the deserted street, a car or two rolled along and broke the silence.

I hadn't said anything, but I suspected another vest had been used, and whoever had had it on was probably nursing a bruise from the .45 slug. I didn't care what Pat said, I could see the trajectory of the slug, and it had traveled straight for the driver's chest. Probably why the car had swerved and not because my bullet had scared them when I hit the trunk. More like it scared them when it hit their chest.

And who was driving the car? Both Marissa and Ellen had been shot and dumped, so either someone was in the car when they went or crawled in when they left. I took another drink and out of the corner of my eye I saw a match flare, the glow of a cigarette being lit and then disappear as a hand closed over it to cover it.

I watched for a few minutes. Whoever was under the awning was good at hiding in the shadows. I stood up again. The butt's glow could barely be seen beneath the cupped hand. I dressed and pulled my piece free of its rig, made sure one was in the chamber, slipped across the room and down the stairs.

Al's shop has a storeroom in the back, lots of cigar boxes and other stuff stacked neat and tidy along the walls. I know Al didn't do it; he was a slob like me, so it had to be Allie. I could hear her chastising him just like Shelly does me when I make a mess. I grinned as I slipped out the back door and down the alley. I kept in the darkness 'til I got to the alley mouth. I could see the man in front of the Busy Bee window. A soft security light way in the back of the store faintly outlined him, but not enough to cut the darkness to see him from the window above.

When he lit another cigarette, I slipped beneath the awning of the hardware store, the shadows deep and dark and all along that side of the street. I moved a couple of stores down and then ran across, hoping the dummy was too interested in the window than in what was going on around him. He was. The only spot lit by moonlight was the small patch between Stevenson's garage and the Busy Bee. I waited and he looked my way once, then looked back to the window.

I bolted across and he saw me, but before he could free his gun, I slammed mine down on his shoulder. He grunted as his rod slipped from his rig and clattered on the concrete.

"Miss the bus?" I asked.

"They ain't no bus --" he stopped himself when I cocked the .45.

"Let's take a walk." I pushed the .45 in his crotch, knelt down and picked up his pistol. His eyes were wide, I stood and motioned for him to start walking.

We made our way down to Fire Station No. 2. The doors were open and the lights out. A couple of firemen sat in chairs and smoked. Jimmy Calhoun was one of the firemen sitting there. I've known him since we were in high school back in St. Lou. Once, when it was hot like this, he told me that he would rather fight fires in the freezing winter than in the summer. At least in the winter you could stay warm fighting the fire, in the summer the heat sapped it all out of you, and he had seen a few guys almost buy it because of heat exhaustion.

He came up out of his chair when he saw the man in front of me walk out into the moonlight, his hands in the air because I had told him to raise 'em.

"What the hell?" Jimmy saw me. He grinned then looked at the other guy in the chair. The other fireman stood, nodded, and went upstairs.

"Trouble, Max?"

"Not yet," I nudged the man toward the firehouse. I think he thought about trying to make a break for it, but Jimmy stepped in front of him. Jimmy stands over six feet tall and is well muscled. His arms looked like they are held together by steel cables. He picked up the chair and waved his hand toward the doorway. The man eyed him, then walked in, Jimmy and I followed. Jimmy sat the chair down by the ladder truck, the sound of wood striking concrete loud in the silence. He sat down on the running board of the engine and crossed his arms over his chest, his arm muscles rippling as he did.

I stood in front of the man. "Now," I shoved him into the chair, "I'm gonna ask you some questions and if I don't get the right answers well..." I looked over to Jimmy and so did the man.

Jimmy gave a big down home grin and clenched one of his fists. The muscles grew underneath the skin into hard cables. His knuckles cracked loudly in the silence. The guy swallowed and looked back at me.

"First, what's your name?"

"Toby."

"Toby what?"

"I want a lawyer!"

"A lawyer. Does this look like a police station?" I glanced at my fireman friend. "Does this look like a police station, Jimmy?"

"Nope, it's a fire station." He glanced around. "Yep, a fire station."

I looked back at the man in the chair. "So I guess those rules for a police station don't apply here, now do they, Toby?"

Toby looked from me to Jimmy. Jimmy's grin turned to a smile and it went from ear to ear.

"Ok Toby, who sent you to keep an eye on me?"

He hesitated and Jimmy made a fist again, this time clenching it hard. I swear I could hear the muscles creak when he did.

Toby fidgeted. "Some guy. He called me, told me just to keep an eye on where you were and what you were up to,"

"Just a guy huh?"

"I swear to God, I don't know who it was!"

"You got a number to call him at if something happens?"

"Yeah, right here."

He reached into his coat and I pressed the muzzle of

the .45 into his forehead. He came out with a piece of paper and handed it to me. I took the gun away and he started to breathe again.

"Thanks." I looked at it and took my gun away from his head. "Now, beat it!"

He looked from me to Jimmy, his mouth open. Jimmy kicked the chair and knocked him over. He fell, then scrambled up to his feet.

"What about my piece?" he asked from the doorway.

I glared at him. "What about it?"

He took off, crossed Commercial and disappeared down Booneville Street in a dead run.

Jimmy laughed and picked up the chair, took it back out and set it in front of the ladder truck.

"Like to sit for a while, Max?" he motioned to the chair.

I nodded as he pulled up another and sat down. "Are you and that other fellow the only ones here?"

"Nope, four others are upstairs playing poker. I'm the lookout this time round.".

I had heard about their midnight poker games and how the fire chief had gotten involved in one and lost his butt. After that there were to be no more poker games, and if caught, suspension. We talked until about three in the morning.

I went back to the apartment, lay on the couch and had been asleep for a few hours when Shelly woke me and told me to get up, Jack was coming home.

CHAPTER 33

Al and I picked up Jack in front of the hospital. A sweet little thing wheeled him out to the car. I pulled Al around to help me load some things in the back while Jack and the nurse eyed each other. She almost kissed him goodbye before she helped him in the car. She held his hand a little longer then she went back inside, looked over her shoulder and disappeared. I chuckled and Al smiled.

"So when're you and her going out?" I asked, looking at him in the rearview.

He shrugged; a lopsided grin crossed his face. "Soon as I call her, which will be very soon,"

Al looked at me and winked. "Did you tell her how big a hero you were in the war?"

"Maybe," Jack's face turned red.

"Sure hope Shelly likes her," I glanced at him again.

"Me too. I mean, why wouldn't she?"

"Did you like me when you first met me?"

"That was different."

"Uh-huh," I said, laughing.

"Those guys that shot me and Shelly, did you get

them?"

"I got one. Right between the eyes."

"Who was he?

"A dirty detective by the name of Perkins."

"So that was you they were talking about."

"Who was talking about?" Al asked.

"One of the doctors and another guy. I was still kinda groggy when they were talking but I did hear the doc say till things were settled, he couldn't do anything else for them."

"Do you remember which doctor?" I asked.

"All I can tell you is he was a short guy."

I nodded, pulled onto Booneville and headed toward home. This was a new twist.

***

I heard Shelly say after we got Jack upstairs and all the hugs and handshakes were done, "Al tells me you met someone?"

Jack looked at Al. His eyes drilled into him. Al snickered.

"Well?" Shelly crossed her arms and stared at Jack. Al had somehow got to Shelly and told her of what we had seen at the hospital. When, I don't know, but he had.

"Look, Shelly…"

"Sit down Jack and let's hear it!"

She was trying not to grin and was doing a pretty damned good job of it. Another side of her I logged away for future reference. Jack sat down on the couch and I headed toward the stairs. He watched me go. I shrugged and exited to the shop downstairs. Allie came up, smiling.

"Did you tell her?" I asked Al once downstairs.

Al laughed and said he did, and I told him Shelly was already grilling him.

"You gonna find out about that number you told me

about?" he asked me.

"Yep." I walked over to the phone and called the switchboard. Betty answered. Betty is one of the girls that is a voice, a sexy voice that brings images of satin legs and deep cleavage.

"Hello Max, honey, long time-no-hear," she said in her sultry tone.

"Hello, Betty, you pretty little thing. I need you to look up a number for me."

"Sure, sugar, what is it?"

I read it off and there was a pause, then she came back.

"It looks as if that number belongs to the secretary's desk of Miss Marissa Clark in the D.A.'s office," she said. "Wasn't she the one who was killed the other night?"

"Yeah, she was. Thanks Betty."

"Anytime, Max. Don't be a stranger, hear?"

She clicked off and I stood looking at the number for a moment.

"Well?" Al asked.

"This number belongs to the phone on desk of Marissa Clark, the woman that was killed." I folded the paper and put it in my pocket. "Last night that hood told me he talked to a man when he called it. Call Pat and tell him what's going on. I'm gonna go over to the hospital and see a short man."

Al nodded and I picked up the phone again, telling Betty to hook him up with Captain Patterson.

***

Wouldn't you know it, the first nurse I saw when I went to ask about the short doctor, was the same one that I told to buzz off when Albert was stabbed. Her name was Velma Stokes and she was hell on wheels when it came to hospital policy.

She was a tall, woman with high cheek bones and full lips. She had hair red as fire, and she was stacked. The only thing that made her a little less appealing was the mean glint she had in her eyes, a stare that could melt holes in steel if she held it on it long enough.

"You again." She put her hands on her hips and give me the stare.

"Yeah." I stared right back. "I'm looking for a doctor, short fellow. He around here somewhere?"

"The only doctor we have around here fitting that description is Doctor Brasher and he's on rounds," she said, not breaking eye contact.

"What floor?" I asked, keeping my eyes steady on her.

"He's on the second floor, west hall. You better not go up there and cause any trouble, you hear me?" She poked a finger in my chest.

"Nope." I broke away and stepped around her. No wonder the one nurse gave me the thumbs up when she passed. The old gal had balls and she didn't mind showing it.

I hopped on the elevator and took it up to the second floor. The doors opened, the quiet broken by squeaky cart wheels and the soft voices of nurses. I stepped off and looked up and down the hallways. A couple of nurses, pretty little things in their starched whites and caps, came toward me.

"There a short doctor running around up here?" If they knew exactly where he was I wouldn't have to hunt him.

"Doctor Brasher." The tall dark headed one fluttered her eyelashes at me as she pointed. "He's down this hallway. Take a right."

"Thanks, sugar." I touched the brim of my hat and both giggled.

I started down the hall and was almost to the turn when Brasher stepped out. He *was* short, probably around five feet tall, and bald as a billiard ball. When he saw me coming his eyes widened. He started to take a step back, then he dropped his clipboard and reached under his coat. My hand dipped under, too, and at the same time we each came out with iron. His fired first, the sound of the pistol loud in the hallway.

I pulled off a shot, but the doc was already in motion, ducking down the hallway. I took off in a run, slid a little as I tried to make the turn on the polished floor. It was a good thing, though, because when I did, he stood about halfway down and popped off another shot. This one whizzed past so close I could feel the heat off of it.

I ducked behind the corner of the hall, waited for another shot and when it didn't come I peeked. The tail of his white coat disappeared down another hall. I made tracks toward him, slowed a little so I wouldn't slide, and flattened myself against the hallway corner. I took a quick peek and noticed the hallway was a dead end. Two doors, one on each side of the hall, showed. I took it slow, inched my way down toward the doors. The one on my left I would try first. By now, I heard the panicked voices of staff and patients.

As I started to try the door, I noticed a window by the right had a door, one with a sliding glass and blinds. The blinds were moving a little. I acted like I was gonna reach for the door knob and then spun. The muzzle of his pistol poked through the blinds. I fired twice. The glass shattered and Doc Brasher fell forward, knocking the rest of the glass out. A piece of it slit his throat as he fell.

So much for talking to him.

CHAPTER 34

After all the questions and statements, Pat and I made our way to City Hall to check Marissa's desk and chat with Carlton again. City Hall used to be the old Federal building and was turned over to the city when the Feds built a new building behind it. Why Carlton had his offices in here instead of the county courthouse was a mystery. Made of granite, it was built on a castle-like design, the front entrance a tall cylinder topped by a dome.

A few years back, one of the weathermen took it upon himself to set up a weather station in the very top of the tower, which was supposed to house a bell. B.J. Wells did his weather forecasts from the bell tower. At first he used a thermometer hung on the stone wall and a wind gauge set in one of the windows. A year later, they installed glass in the three windows and equipment needed to help him forecast the weather. He did so twice a day, with updates when needed.

Pat and I walked into the front entrance and up the stairs to the second floor. Our footsteps echoed on the polished floor. The D.A.'s office was on the east end of the first floor, Carlton's name painted in bold black letters on the door. I swung it open and Pat walked in. I followed.

Pat addressed the new secretary seated at the dead woman's desk. "Carlton in?"

She looked up and Pat flashed his buzzer, then walked to Carlton's door. She looked a little shook and I figured it was because of Pat's serious face and the way he flashed his badge.

"You can't go in until I announce you!" She jumped up from her chair. Pat grunted and opened the door, stopped, then ran in. I followed him and stopped dead.

Carlton's office faced to the south where two big windows looked out onto the city. Carlton sat in his high backed office chair, his head slightly tilted, mouth open. His blood and brains splattered the chair back and some of the upper window behind him.

I turned to tell the secretary to call an ambulance, but she was slumped over her desk. A pinstriped coat tail disappeared out the door. I pulled my piece and ran, hit the door with my shoulder and vaulted into the hall. A man ran as if the devil himself was after him toward the west exit.

I yelled. He stopped and spun around toward me. His hand came up with a pistol. He pulled the trigger and two shots exploded in the hall. People dove for cover. One bullet hit the pillar behind me. The other whizzed close to my ear, very close.

I aimed and pulled the trigger. Two lead missiles cut the air between me and the hood. The man folded in the middle and his gun clattered to the floor. I ran down and kicked his piece to the wall as he fell forward and lay his forehead on the floor. People stuck their heads out of the offices along the hall. I reached down and pushed him over. A grunt came out as his body thumped on the floor, red oozing from between his finger. It was Toby.

"Call an ambulance, Pat!" I yelled as I knelt beside him.

"On its way already." he said, walking up beside me.
"Yeah, just hope they get here before he bleeds out."
They didn't.

CHAPTER 35

Cops found a vest in Carlton's office, my .45 slug embedded in it, a couple of packs of money in his briefcase, and a snub nosed .38 in his hand. The bullet that killed him was a .38 and the gun had been fired. So why didn't anyone in City Hall hear it? I mean, just walking down the hall echoed to beat the band, so a gunshot would have sounded like a small cannon out in the hall, even with the door to the secretary's office closed.

No, this was a set up to look like he had shot himself. The secretary was from the pool Carlton kept. She said the man had gone into Mr. Carlton's office and then came back out...fast. No, she hadn't heard any gunshots. He was about to leave when he came back in, hid in the coat closet, pulled out the gun and told her she was dead if she said a word. When we went in he bolted for the door, rapped her upside the head because she was about to scream. I just happened to see him before he got away. The ambulance attendants checked her out and she went home.

While the boys worked his office, I sat down at Marissa's desk and looked through it. There was the normal office stuff in the drawers. The middle drawer held a wooden tray filled with paper clips, pencils and assorted messages taken a long while back. The left top drawer held a ream of paper and some envelopes. The bottom drawer held a lunch sack and a thermos bottle half filled with coffee. In the right bottom drawer were files. Most of them were cases that had been tried and were ready for their permanent home in the file cabinets down in the basement archives.

Others were letters from people who either thanked him or cursed him. I pulled a few out and read some of them. One thanked Carlton for sending the murderer of her husband to the gas house; another condemned him for sending an innocent man to life in prison.

I then opened the top drawer. A faint, familiar smell wafted, and I moved a couple of papers out of the way. There was a greasy spot under them. I touched it and sniffed.

It was Gun oil, fresh gun oil.

I pulled the drawer out all the way and that was it, nothing but the fresh gun oil. I closed it and sat back in the chair just as Pat came out and leaned against the desk. He sat there for a moment, pulled a cigar from his pocket and clamped down on it.

"Too cut and dried." He switched the cigar from right to left in his mouth.

"Uh-huh, and she didn't have time to see what was in the office because Toby had come back in and threatened her? And if Carlton did kill himself, why didn't she hear the shot?" I watched the attendants leave with Carlton's body bag.

Medical Examiner Pace walked up to us and stripped the rubber gloves from his hands. "I can answer that one."

Pat looked at Pace. "Well?"

"Back in Prohibition Days, one of our D.A.'s was a very careful fellow, his ties with bootleggers a very confidential thing. He was paranoid. He fired and hired a dozen secretaries in a six month period. Claimed each worked for the Feds. He then had his office soundproofed with a hidden exit in case the Feds came after him."

I got up. "Where's this exit?"

Pace motioned for us to follow.

Carlton's office is a pretty nice place, dark wood paneling, carpeted floor and a desk big as a football field. Bookshelves lined three walls with various leather backed books, some of them first editions and very expensive. Pace went over to the bookcase to the right of Carlton's desk and pulled on a piece of molding on the side. There was a click and the bookcase silently opened.

"It leads down to the basement," Pace said, waving toward the entrance, "Enjoy."

He turned and walked out of the office before either of us could ask him how he knew of the passage. Pace had been around a while, so I guess he probably knew a lot of things about this city and its secrets.

I stepped into the passage onto a small landing. Steps went down, another landing turned direction about halfway down. I continued to ascend, Pat followed. A set of footprints were plainly visible in the light of the electric bulbs. I pointed to them and tried not to step in them.

I paused at the turn, a ninety degree job that wasn't as well lighted as the steps coming down from the office. I pulled my .45 loose and stepped around the corner. I could see the basement opening, a black square in the wall. I started down and kept close to the wall. Only one bulb lit the passage, two had burned out. We got close to the basement opening, then stopped and listened. Only silence. Pat tapped my shoulder and I stepped off the last step into the darkness.

It took my eyes a full minute to adjust, but when they did, I saw the dim outlines of boxes and furniture. A boiler sat cold and silent at the south end of the building. A big space had been cleared around it. A workbench stood along the east wall a few feet from the boiler. Old tools lay scattered on it.

We turned and walked toward the north. The dim shape of a door showed, probably leading up into the building. To the left was another stairway, this one leading up. There were windows, but they were covered by boxes stacked to the ceiling. Some showed a bit of light where they had over the years shifted. Not enough to chase away the dark. I walked up to the door and wished I had a flashlight. Pat still right behind me.

I heard a click then Pat whispered, "I found the light switch but it didn't work."

I pushed down on the handle of the door. It moved smoothly and the latch clicked open. I pulled the door open onto a stairwell filled with leaves. Light from the doorway flooded into the basement.

We walked up and looked around. The stairwell led to the east side parking lot. A few cars parked there, most of them labeled as government vehicles. Gas rationing kept most people on foot.

"Dead end." The heat made me sweat. We went back down, leaving the door open for the light, and found why the lights were not working. It was the wrong switch. The one he had clicked operated the door to the passage, the closing so smooth it was silent. We found the right one and clicked on the lights. Dusty bulbs threw off a dim light.

"Small feet and a lot of them; looks like whoever it was came down here a lot," Pat kneeled beside the foot prints we hadn't walked on.

"Yeah," I went to the workbench. A single light hung over it. I took a screwdriver and poked around on the bench. Dust, tools and nothing else. The boiler was shut down for the summer, the door closed and latched. Why, I don't know, but I grabbed the latch and opened the door. I grinned and called to Pat. He came over and let out a low whistle. Packets of bills, ten rows high and ten rows across sat just in the opening of the boiler. They were all hundreds.

I pulled a couple out of one of the bundles. "Hell of a safe."

"Safe, or pick up spot," he said. "Wonder where they keep it in the winter?"

"I wonder if the maintenance man here is part of the deal." I put one of the bills back, the other one I held for a moment, the feel of it funny. As I closed the boiler door I slipped the bill in my pocket, Pat closed the outside door. We walked back up to the office, then out into the building and looked for the man who kept the facilities going.

Jobe Miller was his name and he was leaving the building on the west side. Pat called to him. He acted like he didn't hear. Pat yelled again and he bolted. He was halfway to the door, looking back, when one of the women who worked there stepped out into the hall. He slammed into her and Pat was on him in a minute. I helped the young lady out of the way while Pat slammed the guy face first onto the floor and pushed his knee into his back.

"Going someplace?" Pat said as he clicked the cuffs on Jobe and then turned him over on his back. The guy spit in Pat's face and Pat slugged him, square in the mouth, bouncing his head off the polished, marble floor. Two uniforms came and picked him up. Jobe's head flopped around on his shoulders.

"Take him to the Station," Pat said. "Book him for assault."

I watched Pat wipe his face with a hanky then ask the girl if she was all right. She said she was then walked away, adjusting her clothes as she went.

"Coming?" I asked as he watched the swing of her butt.

He looked at me and gave a sheepish grin.

"Old buddy, you need to get around more often,

maybe take in some sights like that one." He looked at me, mumbled under his breath and turned to go. The door to the office opened again. Pat pulled up, but not in time. I walked past him and snickered as he pulled himself loose from the woman and apologized.

***

"Assault!" the man named Jobe almost screamed, "I didn't assault anyone!"

"Then what's this lump on my jaw?" Pat leaning over the table, his eyes locked on Jobe's, his voice low but level. "You were running, in flight, I yelled halt and you grabbed a woman. She tripped you up and I caught you, then you slugged me. Now, if I talked to her just right, I think she would be willing to file charges against you." He looked in my direction. "Don't you think so, Max?"

"Yeah, I do believe she would." I watched Jobe. He was skinny man. His shoulder joints showed through like knobs under this thin shirt. His face was long and gaunt, his lips thin. His hair was nothing but little wisps on top of his head and on the sides. His fingers were long, thin, and calloused.

"So." Pat leaned back, his eyes still locked once again on Jobe. "Where did the money in the boiler come from?"

His eyes grew big, he laced and unlaced his fingers, his face paled.

"Well?" Pat leaned forward again, growling out the word.

"I don't know nothing about no money!" Jobe answered in a shaky voice

"You don't, huh. I bet if we took one of your shoes and matched them with the footprints we found..." Pat leaned in close. His eyes flashed and a wicked grin stretched across his lips. He was bluffing. Jobe's shoes were number ten or larger.

"I don't know who it was. I caught them counting it and stuffing it in a valise. I asked about it and was told to mind my own business, that it was campaign money to be shipped out."

"Didn't it seem kind of funny that campaign money was kept in a boiler, Jobe?" I asked him. He shrugged.

"Shipped out to where?" Pat continued.

"Different places I guess. I didn't ask."

"Come on Jobe, fess up, man." Pat leaned even closer to Jobe. Any closer and he could give him a kiss. "You know the money wasn't contributions. In fact, I bet you know exactly what the money was for, don't you?"

"I don't know, okay? That woman—" He stopped, fear in his eyes.

I rubbed my hands together like I was really getting pissed. "A woman, huh? You led us to believe it was a man, how did you know?"

"She smelled of a fancy perfume. The kind my wife samples when she is at the department store."

"Are you sure it wasn't Carlton's secretary?"

He looked at me and shook his head. "Uh-uh, she was taller than her."

I stood, walked around to where he was, sat down on the edge of the table and tipped my fedora back. "We know Carlton didn't shoot himself, Jobe, but I suspect you know that, too. I suspect you have known about this secret passage to Carlton's office for a long time. You caught this person taking money out of the boiler and threatened to turn them in. They fed you a story they were being blackmailed into helping Carlton dispose of the money and if you would help them, they would cut you in. Am I right?" I watched his eyes for a clue, anything that would give him away.

He glanced up at me, then down, his fingers lacing and unlacing again. "Damn it! Yeah," he said in a low voice, "She told me there would be more money than I could imagine if I helped her. I was told to keep it there and keep my mouth shut, she'd be back soon to split the money with me."

"She say when she would be back?"

"A few days from now. That's all."

"Describe her." Pat leaned back a little, his eyes were like drill bits.

Jobe swallowed and glanced up ant Pat then back down again before he spoke. "She was small, came up to my shoulders, I never seen her face cause she had on one of those wide brimmed fedoras and a scarf wrapped around her mouth that hid the rest of her face. She always wore gloves. She talked funny too, like she had a mouth full of something."

I walking back to my chair. "So let me see if I have this straight." I sat down. "You happen to be down in the basement one day looking around and you catch someone getting ready to load the money from the boiler. They make a deal with you, one that promises a lot of cash if you will just do what they tell you, or they will turn you in, and with your record it could go hard for you."

"How did you know...?"

"I didn't, but your eyes told me so the minute I mentioned it. They then told you that all you needed to do was keep the cash here 'til all was quiet then they would split it with you." I paused and Jobe just sat staring, his mouth open.

"Then you hear about the murder of Carlton today and you begin to sweat. You decide to go around to the side and come into the basement from the stair well, maybe take a little money out so you can disappear. But that doesn't go well because you see me and Pat coming out the door there. You go back in and try to look invisible. But you get antsy, decide that the money wasn't worth it and try to leave. In the meanwhile, me and Pat here have been looking for you and we find you and well, here we are."

I leaned on the table. "Am I right?"

Jobe just sat staring, his hands doing the lacing thing. There was a knock on the door and a detective came in, handed Pat a file and left. Pat opened it and scanned it for a second. The corners of his mouth turned up.

"Well, Jobe," Pat said, looking at him. "Looks like you have a few marks against you. Petty theft, assault twice, drunk and disorderly more than a few times, attempted robbery, which was the one that you spent eighteen months in the pen for."

"So now we can put murder on there, or at least accessory to murder," I added.

"I didn't kill anyone!" Jobe said.

"Well, I mean if I am correct on my estimations, then I suspect you will go down for it unless…." I let my words trail off and Jobe looked at me, his mouth trembling, his hands shaking.

"Help us out and I'll put a word in for you," Pat said, eyeing him.

"They were supposed to come back in a few days; they said that that would be enough time for things to cool off. They said they would contact me and I am to meet them in the boiler room, the money divided and then we disappear." he finished.

"Okay" I gave an even bigger grin. "Let's see that they aren't disappointed."

CHAPTER 36

It was all set and unless the party in question was aware of Jobe having been caught we might be able to end this case, and none too soon. I was tired and I missed Shelly. This had been a real roller coaster ride, lots of bodies had piled up and probably still more before it was over. Someone was cleaning up loose ends and doing a damned good job of it! Just about everyone involved in one way or the other had been eliminated.

We had informed Agent Trent of what we were up to and he had sent a couple of his boys to back us up. Trent said he had to go to St. Louis on urgent business. I was perched in the passage. The mechanism holding the door was closed unhooked so I could hide in the darkness of the doorway with the door partly shut. Pat and another agent had found a spot around behind the boiler. The light bulb back there unscrewed, the two of them hidden in the dark.

Still, I had a bad feeling. Why would the other party agree to a split unless Jobe had been in on the deal? He swore he wasn't but his story was thin, even Pat said so. Still, there was the chance it wasn't and we were taking that chance.

Sometimes you have to or things will just drag on and on like they were doing now, and I'm not one to drag it out. I wanted the head honcho bad so I could maybe give him a little of what his boys had given me. I settled in and waited.

The sun had just set when Jobe came down to the basement carrying a leather valise. He set it on the tool bench and opened the door to the boiler. He stepped back, his eyes wide and his mouth working. I'll admit, we didn't check the boiler and we should of, which was maybe a good thing because when Jobe turned to run, I caught the whiff of gas. Then the boiler fired off, three feet of hot flame enveloped Jobe. His clothes, already greasy, ignited and fried him good.

I jerked the passage door open and stepped out. Pat and the agent scrambled from behind the boiler. Pat looked for the cut off to the gas and found that the handle was gone.

Flames still belched from the boiler, and I noticed that they crawled along the boxes stored there. I yelled to Pat and the agent to get the hell out!

The agent was trying to put out the fire on Jobe. I yelled to him it was too late. The boiler belched another ball of flame out. The agent flattened on the floor; the fire scorched his back and hat. He was up in a heartbeat and ran toward us as we ran up the stairs to the opening in Carlton's office.

I pulled the lever that operated the door and it clicked, but nothing happened. I pulled again, still nothing. The third time, Pat and the agent leaned on the bookcase. It moved about an inch. Smoke and heat filled the passage as the boxes burned below. I gave it another hard pull and the bookcase slid open. Smoke poured into the office. The agent ran to the desk and picked up the phone to call it in. It didn't work. All three of us headed for the doors.

I could hear the boiler rumbling, could feel it through

the floor. Pat hit the door and we were outside. A couple of passing cops heard the explosion and came at a run. They helped us down to the street. One of them had called in the blast and Number 2 Fire Station was on the way.

I took in some deep breaths and coughed a bit, then turned to face City Hall. The basement windows glowed. Smoke bellowed and people bailed out of the building. I leaned against the car behind me and shook my head. This was going to end, and I was gonna end it hard.

***

While I was in the emergency room, I pulled out the bill I had liberated on our first run of the basement because something wasn't right about it. As I looked it over, I knew then what was going on and that Jobe had been set up. I left the emergency room and headed to Samson's building again, this time with a fist full of knuckles if Lenny gave me any crap! Samson had to know more than he was telling.

A man in his business kept his eye on the ones who ran things on the edge of his territory, or had made a deal with him to stay out of his business and just run their own. I figured that was what had happened and he ignored them and stayed clear, let them make their own mistakes that would get them caught.

I pulled into the parking lot and vacated the car. My hand dipped under my coat and pulled the .45 from its home. I pushed the door buzzer. It sounded loud in the building. In two seconds I pushed it again and again. Someone cussed and I could hear heavy footsteps approaching.

Lenny opened the door and when he did, I shoved the .45 under his chin, grinning like a maniac. I pushed him back inside. He stuttered a couple of words and I told him to swallow them, I wanted to see Samson and right now!

He gave me a bad look. I cocked the .45 and that look disappeared.

The warehouse was empty. I was lucky because if there had been a few men there I would have had to pop Lenny and a few of them to get to Sampson. Lenny backed toward the door and I stopped when he backed into it. I told him to turn slow and open the door, not to enter, just open it and be a good boy. He did, and before he could move, I whacked him on the head with my .45, shoved him to the side and slammed the door shut. I stepped inside and wedged a chair under the door handle, just in case. I crossed the room and Samson's door opened. He stood there, a big smile on his face.

"I have been expecting you, Max." He motioned me in.

I stepped in and he closed the door, walked past me and sat down at his desk. My .45 was still cocked and ready.

"No need for that, Max." He opened his humidor and offered me a cigar. I shook my head and walked over to him, keeping one of the chairs in front of his desk between us.

"Please," he said, motioning to the .45. "If you have something to say, say it, but without the artillery."

I took the bill from my coat pocket and tossed it on his desk before I slid my piece home and sat down. He picked it up and looked at it closely. His hand went in and came out of his desk with a magnifying glass.

"My, my," he said, and put the glass down. "This is almost as good as the treasury puts out."

"What the hell is going on, Samson?" I eyed him, not breaking contact. "First I'm told about this white slavery ring operating here in our backyard and then I come across a boiler full of money that it isn't real money."

"So it would seem." Samson leaned back in his chair. "Max, let me assure you, I have nothing to do with this.

This is not the agreement I made with them."

"What did you agree to, then?" I said, leaning forward.

"I was told that shipments would be coming into Ava's place, picked up and then money delivered and dispersed. I never asked what the shipments were because it came from the east, I was told to ignore it. I suspected things. That was why Benny had sided with them, and it was from him I found out what was going on. He was to learn more but, alas, you ended that little spy game when he crossed your path."

I shrugged and he smiled. I guess my record had been broken, at that.

"I would say," he continued, "That this is an attempt to clean up things before they pull out and move elsewhere and start again. Simply disappear. I'd say Carlton and his confidant realized that the last few payoffs were this funny money and they were trying to keep from getting busted, as the police say. I assume the money in the boiler was destroyed in the blast?"

I nodded.

"Then I'd look to the origin of this business, as we call it. I would say that there are some loose ends that will have to be tied up there, also," Samson said. He motioned toward the door. I stood and looked at the door, then back to Samson.

"Oh, don't worry about Lenny; he has been listening as we talked. He won't bother you when you leave. I just wouldn't encounter him in any dark alleys, if I were you, any time soon." He chuckled and pushed a button on the intercom.

I walked out of the office and out to my car. Lenny stood in the dock doorway and pointed a finger at me like a gun. He let his thumb fall.

CHAPTER 37

They were trying to leave clean, Samson had said to me. They planned to kill off all those involved, especially those that might be able to hang the ball and chain around their necks. But who? They wanted us to believe it was Carlton and that he had blown his head off when we were getting too close. But we hadn't bought it, and so when we cornered Jobe, they had tried again. And failed again. I leaned back in my chair and stared at the office ceiling. The cracks were the same as had been there an hour ago. The fly specks on the white of the paint had always been there.

A lot of people had died because of greed and money. I had been shot at and beaten because of it, as had my friends and the one I loved. The money was a sidetrack, the diversion to make us believe it was Carlton and his secretary who was in thick with them.

Or was it?

Carlton had probably spotted the funny money and blamed it on the New York bunch, and they in turn had told him that someone was playing him. So he went to the head honcho and made a threat. Then they blow his head off and make it look like suicide.

But I wasn't buying it. When the Medical Examiner told us about the secret passage, they knew we would round up the janitor, set up a trap and try and nail them. But it wasn't the type of trap the janitor expected. In fact, he was just another person to be eliminated because he might have recognized the person he had talked to in the boiler room.

Pat had told me it was an incendiary bomb. The boiler was one of the new gas types. They unhooked the gas line and the bomb was wired to the door so that when it opened, the bomb went off. The second blast was from a rupture in the line running up to the boiler. I laced my fingers together and used them as a pillow while I leaned back.

Counterfeiting?

No, that would have been caught in a few months around here. The people here might be thought of as hicks back east, but they ain't stupid. A couple of local fellows tried to make their own green, and after a month, they were sitting in the state pen, the Feds having–. "That's it."

I let my feet slip off the table and onto the floor. My shoes thumped the wood, hard. The Feds had taken the funny money, which one of the agents said was very, very good, to the Federal Building where it was supposed to be destroyed. I grinned, stood, grabbed my .45 and slipped it home then called Pat and told him to meet me at Al's.

CHAPTER 38

I told Al and Pat what I suspected. Pat tossed a file on the counter. He had been thinking along the same lines and had done some digging.

Seems the distillery business wasn't all that the real Gates brothers were into. Daddy had been a bootlegger from the get go. When the Volstead Act was repealed, he applied for a liquor license and had been granted said license after calling in a few favors from the men in the state house. Those he had called the favors from had been his best customers.

It was an all in the family thing. The boys made the hooch and Becky opened a speakeasy/ bordello. Young girls shipped up to her house and trained during their period there, then shipped out to other houses they ran across the county.

Somewhere along the line, the New York boys had gotten a hold of the old man and tried to convince him that he would be a lot better off if he threw in with them. I mean, they were making a killing all around the county and the New York boys wanted a part of it, just like they had taken a part of a few others down through the other states.

The old man told them to go to hell and if they tried anything, they would be sorry. Well, they did, and they were sorry. A car load of hoods were found in a wooded area, cut to ribbons by automatic machine gun fire. Of course the local law passed it off as hill justice and didn't look any farther, but they knew who had blasted the hoods.

It was later the old man was found blasted to death with shotguns and his car set on fire. The New York boys had sent their warning.

The brother's and Becky agreed to send one of their own to New York to make peace. New York asked for Becky to be sent to negotiate. They sent her.

However, unbeknownst to her brothers, Becky had made a deal with the boys in New York on the sly, even before their daddy was killed. Once she left, they didn't see her again.

Becky met Mario Antonalli, who set her up in a 'house', the same business she had managed before, for her family. She was good at it, but she didn't want to do it using her real name, afraid someone would find her, so she went under the name of Ava Peasant. The face alteration was included with Mario's bankrolling the business.

However, things changed. Mario fell, blown away, and the house was taken over by Sal Taylor. Sal took a liking to Ava instantly. She was brazen and tough, just the kind of girl he looked for to run a different kind of house. One in Springfield. One for his drug distribution point and bordello.

So Sal set Becky/Ava up, sent her down here and paid off certain officials to keep them from getting nosy. It was her brothers who got nosey. A cousin, who lived north of town, recognized her and sent word back. The boys hired a detective, he came down and disappeared, as did the cousin. Then the brothers died in an accidental boiler blast.

Pat commented on *that* blast being written up as an

accident, but the one that happened here, he doubted was an accident at all.

This file held a lot of information. Some of it being that somewhere in there Ava met Agent Trent, and it was Trent who talked Becky/Ava into the white slavery business. Of course, Sal got wind of what they were doing and confronted them. Trent almost bought the farm 'til Sal realized how much money they were making. He made a deal with them, sixty percent of the take and they could live. They chose to live.

"It says here Trent was supposed to be working under cover for the Feds," I said after I finished reading the file, "Somewhere along the line he turned. Hell, he even wrote the report."

"Considering the average salary for an agent is a little under five grand a year, who could blame him," Pat retorted. "They were taking in over three million a year."

I placed to folder on the counter. "Could you do it?" A frown crossed his face and he started to answer until Al cut him off.

"So Trent and Ava have been the brains behind this all along?" Al leaned on the counter and read some more.

Pat lit a stogie. "I'm not so sure." He leaned against the case, the argument stopped before it got started. "Carlton was getting updates from him and, I do believe, passing them on to someone else. That someone else being the one really in command."

I looked at Pat. "And I bet I have a good idea who it is."

"Yeah, she is probably the one who you saw exiting the diner," Pat said. "And she was probably in the car to take care of business when the delivery was made at the house. Either way, Ava was a subordinate. But where does the counterfeit money come in?"

I shrugged. I had an idea where it figured in but wasn't going to tell just yet.

"So what you wanna do Pat?" Al closed the file.
"Bust the bastards," he said in a low voice.
Al and I both nodded.

CHAPTER 39

I loaded the last of my clips and sat back in my chair and thought over what was and what wasn't. This whole thing started as a simple trace, a couple of fellows who had come looking for a girl that wasn't their sister; two men, one who had died, the other almost. Shelly, and Jack had almost gotten taken out, and me also. All because of money and greed.

I slipped the two clips in my jacket pocket, checked my .45 and made sure one was in the chamber. I wanted this first one to be all Trent's. I grabbed my hat and started for the door. My hand was about to turn the knob when the floor beneath me shook and there was a cough, then a boom that tossed me back and onto the floor. I grabbed the knob and wrenched the door open just in time to see flames blast out of Al's shop.

I ran. The flames roared from the inside of the shop. The upstairs caved in. I yelled, tried to go in, but the fire was too hot. I tried again and someone grabbed me and held me back. I turned and Jack stood there, his face smeared with soot and his eyes narrowed and filled with anger.

"Max," he yelled, "Max, Shelly's okay. Shaken, but ok."

"Al...."

He shook his head and I went with him to where Shelly was on the sidewalk. She saw me and dove into my arms. Her face was smeared with soot and there was a cut over her eye. I held her for a long time, and as I held her I looked at Jack with a question in my eye.

"We were on the fire escape talking because of the heat. I started to get up and go back in when the whole inside of the room heaved up and fell in. The boom followed after and the concussion almost knocked us both off the fire escape. I told Shelly to grab the ladder and hold on. We both went down together and had maybe gotten a foot past the escape, when it came loose from the wall and fell," he said as fire trucks from the No. 2 fire station screamed to a halt and unrolled hoses.

"Al and Allie were down in the shop. Some guy delivered a package while we were having supper and they went down to see what it was," Jack finished.

"This ends tonight," I hissed. I helped Shelly to the ambulance that had just pulled up. She wouldn't let go of me until I pried her loose.

"Max, please don't go!" she cried. I sat down and held her. Pat and his men pulled up. His face was long and deadly. Shelly was in shock and they needed to take her to the hospital to keep watch on her. I nodded and crawled in with her. I held her hand and told her I would be back soon, that I needed to end this tonight.

She nodded and I stepped down from the ambulance as Pat told one of the patrolmen that if anything happened to her, he would make sure his life was a living hell as long as he was a cop. The man nodded and pulled a .45 auto from his belt. Pat slapped him on the shoulder.

"Got another one of those?" Jack asked. Pat looked at

me and I nodded. We walked over to his car and he pulled another .45 out and a couple of clips. Jack stuck the .45 in his waistband and crawled in the back. He picked up the shotgun, leaned against the car and looked it over, then rested it between his legs. I crawled in beside Pat as he started the cruiser up, slipping it into gear, and headed south.

"Trent is mine," I said in a low voice.

"Trent?" Pat looked over at me. I nodded and we drove on in silence.

CHAPTER 40

We parked just before the rise in the road. Jack slid out of the car in a crouch and made his way up to the crest, then into the brush, silent as a shadow. The war taught him real good.

We followed him. There was a lot of activity going on down at Ava's. Men went in and out, laughing and slapping each other on the backs. We cut across the open clearing and into the brush again. Jack went ahead, doing what he would call recon. One of the hoods walked around the edge of the yard, smoking a cigarette and watching the road. He would never get to do that again.

Jack moved on toward the house. Another hood took a piss by the wood pile. Jack sent him to meet St. Peter. I mounted the steps, was halfway up when the door opened and a fellow with a pencil mustache staggered out. He took the butt of my .45 right between the eyes, grunted, and we quietly eased him to the ground. I stepped into the kitchen. It was a small room with a wood cook stove that looked like it had seen better days, a table piled up with whiskey bottles, and a passed out hood in one of the chairs.

Jack wanted to slit his throat but we stopped him, told him to watch the door. Pat and I worked on him. He came to after a couple of pitchers of water and a slap in the face. His hands came up to wipe out his eyes. There was a powder burn in the web of his right hand. His first sight when he lowered his hands was the .45 muzzle staring him in the eyes. He blinked, started to yell, and I pushed the muzzle into his mouth.

"Not a good thing to do," I said. He looked down at the gun in his mouth then back at me. He started to shake. When I wiggled the gun, he pissed himself.

"I'm gonna ask you a question," I hissed in his face, "and when I pull this piece out of your mouth, you better answer as quiet as possible, ok?"

He nodded.

"Is Trent here?" I pulled the piece out of his mouth. He coughed and nodded his head.

"Where?" I was like a snake ready to strike.

"Cellar," he croaked. "With Miss Ava."

"Thanks." I slammed the muzzle of the .45 on top of his head. He went out again.

I told Jack to keep an eye out, and if anything happened, to blow a path out of here. He nodded and watched the festivities through a crack in the door. I went to the cellar door, then stopped.

Pat was behind me. "What?"

"We both go down these stairs, we both are in the line of fire."

"I'll take the outside cellar entrance," he offered.

I waved my hand at Jack. He looked at me and I silently mouthed, "Go with Pat."

He nodded and they left out the back entrance. I gripped the door knob and started to open it when the door to the main parlor opened wide. The cutie named Elsa pointed a .32 automatic at my head.

"Hello, Max," she said in a sexy voice.

I stood with my .45 ready. The corners of her mouth turned up.

"Looks like we have a Mexican standoff here." She was dressed the same way I had seen her when she had rounded the corner of the diner.

"Except my Mexican is bigger than yours," I waved the muzzle of my .45 at her.

"So it is," she replied. "I saw your man peek into the parlor. I could have popped him then, but I figured you were close. I mean, Trent has gotten sloppy."

"Yeah he has, hasn't he? He tells me you take orders pretty well." I baited her.

"Take orders, hell," she spat at me. "I'm the one who gives the orders to him!"

"Not the way he tells it," I argued, shaking my head. Her face went red and she grunted, muttering something about a son of a bitch under her breath.

"Well, it really doesn't matter because he..."

Suddenly, gunshots boomed from the cellar and Jack yelled.

I dove to the floor just as Elsa pulled the trigger. The slug burned a path across the back of my coat. I started to put a couple in her when the cellar door exploded off its hinges, scraped a path across my back and slammed into Elsa full force. A ball of flame scorched the door and her. When the door fell, she fell with it. Her head split open from the impact. Her eyes went wide and empty. Flames roared up the stairs as the old wood in the basement caught. I pulled myself up and staggered to the kitchen door, Smoke billowed behind me as I bolted through.

"OUT!" I yelled, but people were already moving. Smoke from the basement billowed from the kitchen into the room. I grabbed one of the girls and asked who was upstairs.

"A couple of girls, and–. She bolted out the door.

"Shit!" I mounted the stairs, then fired the .45 three

times and heads poked out of two doorways, one of them a man, a city favorite.

"FIRE!" That was all it took. They bolted out of the house, the city favorite naked as the day he was born. Flames already crawled across the ceiling in the living room, the heat sucked sweat out of me as I ran. Pat and Jack were already around front. The house went up quick, flames now bursting through the upstairs windows.

"Trent?" I asked.

"He came out of the basement quick." Jack huffed to catch his breath. "The blast knocked us both over and tossed Trent out into the yard. Before I could get up, he was in the brush. I heard a car start. I didn't get there fast enough, he was gone."

"Ava was she–"

"She never came out, Max," Pat said, shaking his head.

"Damn." I coughed then sat down on the grass. My lungs burned from the smoke.

Pat pulled some keys out of his pocket. "We better go get the car."

I nodded and then started to laugh. Pat looked at me like I was crazy until I pointed. The city's favorite was coming toward us. He had on one of the girl's thin robes. Pat smiled and went for the car.

When Jack and I started to follow Pat, the man raised his hand to stop us. "Ah, h-hey, fella's, think you can, a-ah, give me a li, well a lift? I'd really like to get out of here before the reporters come."

Jack laughed and so did I. The poor guy looked pitiful in pink. I motioned him forward. "Come on. If I were you, I wouldn't want to be caught in that outfit either."

His eye's lost their worried look. "Thanks!"

I knew he wasn't married. Lucky for him because a wife would have been pretty peeved when he explained why he came home like that.

CHAPTER 41

I had Pat drop me off close to the office and told him to take Jack to see about his sister. He nodded. I watched them leave and then tried the door latch. I knew the door would be unlocked, and I knew who unlocked it.

See, I had helped destroy a perfectly good racket, tied into New York, for a man and his whore. Yeah, and he was gonna try to make damned sure I paid for it. I couldn't see Sal being involved in the counterfeiting business. It had to be Trent and Trent alone who was shifting the funny money for the real thing, and like Sampson said, it was good enough to be real so nobody had caught it yet.

I turned the knob and stepped in, my .45 cocked and ready. The light was on in my office. As I gripped the knob and pushed the door open, I saw him in my chair, the back of his clothes still smoking.

"Hello, Trent," I walked in and stood in front of my desk.

He coughed, and then pumped a shell in the shotgun he had aimed at my head. "I figured you'd go see the love of your life first," he wheezed.

He was in pain, his face showed it. I could of ducked inside fast and taken him out, but I wanted to hear his explanation about the funny money. "Nope, figured to come and see you."

He raised the shotgun. "The piece. Put it on the desk."

I shrugged and laid it down. He leaned forward, grabbed it, let the hammer down then tossed it back on the desk, away from me. I caught a whiff of burned flesh and burned cloth as he moved. He winced when he leaned back.

" Sorry about Ava?" I asked, watching him.

"A casualty of the trade," he said through clenched teeth. "She had to be eliminated, but not in the way Sal wanted me to do it."

"Oh?"

"She was someone I_cared about, Black. We were gonna disappear together when we had this all settled." He flinched in pain. "Maybe Mexico or South America where we could start over. Sal wanted me to kill her. He knew we were sleeping together and it pissed him off. She's gone now so...."

He sucked in a deep breath, then let it out slowly. The action made him groan.

"What about Elsa?" I locked eyes with him.

He shrugged. "She only thought she was in charge." He fought to catch his breath. "I let her think she was. She was one of our best at prepping the girls who came in. Then she and that Marissa woman got greedy. Even that bitch, Ellen, scammed us." His brow furrowed. "And don't think I didn't know you caught that Ellen hadn't said anything about the pickups. I knew you knew. Anyway, Sal told me to let it continue. Said when the time came, he'd take care of both of 'em."

He shook his head, the look of disbelief and contempt in his eyes. "But, then you come along and screw everything up by taking in those two idiots acting as the Gates brothers. Something had to be done. I knew you would find out sooner or later what was going on."

"Yeah, well, you crossed the line didn't you Matt. Crossed it way back when you tried to kill Shelly and my friends.".

He shot me a crooked smirk. "Oh, speaking of friends, did they get the little package I had sent?"

This time the contempt was on my face I clenched my fists and edged toward him. He fired a shot at the wall close to me. The sound was deafening in the small room. "The line? That put you way over," I hissed.

He held the gun steady. "Like I said, you should have given it up and maybe those friends would still be alive."

I locked eyes with him and he smirked again, the gun pointed directly at me. I pulled my coat open. Slowly, my hand went to my shirt pocket and pulled out the bill Sampson had looked at and given back to me.

"What about the funny money?" I tossed it on the desk. "Does Sal know about that?"

Trent laughed, winced, then tried to stifle a coughing fit. He hawked then spit, the spittle tinted red. "Not at first. Carlton figured that one out. He called Elsa and confronted her about it. She told him not to worry, that it was all being taken care of, that the last payoff was sent and it was let slip that he was the one switching the money. Poor fool couldn't take a chance on you figuring out he had lied about it so he confronted Elsa. She blew his brains out and made it look like a suicide. What she didn't count on was someone knowing about the passage down to the basement from his office, and you two finding the money."

"So was it your idea or Elsa's to launder the counterfeit money through Sal and his banks?"

"Since you asked, it was. The money came from a bust up in Kansas City, some of it from here. Some small timers who did excellent work got nabbed and a friend of mine told me about the money. He was the one who said it would be funny if someone tried to launder through Sal's organization to set him up for a bust. I talked to my supervisor and he thought it was a good idea since I was working both sides, bust up Sal's whore operation and also get him for counterfeiting."

"So let me get this straight," I continued to watch him. His face was tight with pain and his breathing, labored. "The payoff money was picked up by Marissa and taken to the boiler room where she replaced it with the counterfeit money, then sent it on. Looks like Sal would have gotten wise to it."

"Yeah, he did. At first we only replaced a few packets of money at a time, then Marissa got greedy and replaced more. One of Sal's boys caught it and sent word down about it. Elsa took care of her that night she and Ellen went for the pickup. Elsa told them she needed to go back into town with them and see me."

Things were becoming more clear. I pieced it together in my head. "I see, and Jobe, how was he a part of this?"

"Just another casualty in the wrong place at the wrong time. He happened on the money before we could get rid of all of it. Elsa was there loading some of it in a valise when he caught her. Threatened to turn her in until she promised him half the swag and some extras. He didn't know the money was funny. He went right along with it. But again, enter *Max Black*! She knew you would get the deal out of him so she set up the hit. I gotta tell you, you are the luckiest bastard I have ever known."

I lifted my shoulders in a shrug. What else could I do? I knew he was right. "Go on."

"Then I learned that Elsa told Sal that it was me who instigated the money switch. I had to do something, especially since the operation was going bust. I was going to tell Ava to pack her bags, we were going to get the hell out of Dodge before the shit hit the fan, but—"

Damn, was that a tear I saw in the bastard's eye. "But what?"

Ava was dead, shot in the head before your guys got there. I was going back out when that cop, and the other guy, busted through the cellar doors. While I was hauling ass out of there, the bomb, probably set by Elsa, went off." He wiped his cheek with the back of his hand. "She knew Ava and I were going to meet down there tonight. Elsa felt betrayed. You coming along was just an added dividend which she hoped would pay off."

I shifted my weight from one foot to the other. "So why didn't she let me go on down?"

"Who knows, she had been a little bit loopy these past few days, maybe she wanted the pleasure of putting one between your eyes."

"Well, she didn't. Looks like you didn't fair to well either." I inched forward a bit.

"Oh, I will survive this. I have a lot of money socked away, and a way out."

He coughed again, this time his lips became covered with bloody spit.

"And that way out is?"

"Why, the drunk passed out down in the basement beside Ava. I dragged him down from the party, put my badge and ID on him. Well, Max, there you have it, not a good ending but one that I think I can live with, so goodbye, shamus."

He raised the shotgun and I tensed for a dive toward him. He grinned and then his grin fell as his eyes cut toward the door behind me, then I heard Jack's voice.

"Shamus my ass, good bye Trent!"

Trent jerked the shotgun toward Jack. The kid ducked out of the doorway as he pulled the trigger, I lunged to the side. A .45 slug went wide and slammed into the wall above Trent's head. Trent fired off a shot and the door jamb to my office tossed splinters Jack's way. I was almost to my .45 still lying on my desk. Trent cussed and swung the trench gun toward me. But he wasn't quick enough. I had already wrapped my fingers around the butt of my gun. I pulled the trigger and two .45 slugs slammed into him. The last one blew the top of his head off and dropped him to the floor.

CHAPTER 42

I wish I could say that things were going to be all right, but they weren't. We had lost some good people to this bunch of hoods, one in particular. Al was buried with full honors and his wife lay beside him. Both will be missed, especially the cigar shop which was to have been his relaxation. Jack mentioned he might rebuild or open another, but that would have to come after he was done with the army and their push for people.

Al had insured the business and the money went to Jack and Shelly. She placed it in a savings account for when Jack decided what he wanted to do. Jack shipped out after the funeral and told me to be good to his sister or he would come back and kick my ass. His grin told me he knew me and Shelly would be okay.

Shelly and I talked about marriage, but neither one of us wanted to push the other. I guess maybe after what had happened, she wanted to think it over some more. I solved that by presenting her with a ring. Just a simple engagement job. She cried so hard I thought maybe she was gonna say no. Then she laid one on me and whispered in my ear, "Yes."

I felt like the king of the world. Life is too short to hedge, and that was what we were both doing. Now if we can just decide on a date.

The heat was still around and Cooney was still saying he would get to the fan. He did, all right 'bout the time the heat spell broke and it cooled off. You should have seen the look on his face the day he came to fix it. My Shelly wore a button up shirt and a pair of slacks. That was very disappointing that day for said landlord.

ABOUT THE AUTHOR

Author Ike Keen

Ike Keen likes the tough guys. So tough guys are what he writes about.

He has been writing since 1986 and started off in the horror field. He's had short stories published in Fright Depot, Sterling Web and Black Pedals. However, soon he decided to go a different route by trying his hand in hardboiled detective stories. Mickey Spillane and Max Allen Collins are a couple of his favorite authors. He's adapted to that old school style, and made it his own.

Retired from the Springfield Public Schools, he now lives in a rural Missouri town. He hopes to include the setting in one of his future novels.

Keep an eye out for the next two novel's in the Max Black series.

www.ingramcontent.com/pod-product-compliance
Lightning Source LLC
Chambersburg PA
CBHW061159170626
46809CB00003B/1165